A DUKE'S GUIDE TO ROMANCE

THE GENTLEMEN AUTHORS

SOPHIE BARNES

A DUKE'S GUIDE TO ROMANCE

The Gentlemen Authors

Copyright © 2023 by Sophie Barnes

Cover Design by The Killion Group, Inc.

ALSO BY SOPHIE BARNES

Novels

The Gentlemen Authors
A Duke's Guide To Romance

Brazen Beauties
Mr. West and The Widow
Mr. Grier and The Governess
Mr. Dale and The Divorcée

Diamonds in the Rough
The Dishonored Viscount
Her Scottish Scoundrel
The Formidable Earl
The Forgotten Duke
The Infamous Duchess
The Illegitimate Duke
The Duke of Her Desire
A Most Unlikely Duke

The Crawfords
Her Seafaring Scoundrel

More Than a Rogue

No Ordinary Duke

Secrets at Thorncliff Manor

Christmas at Thorncliff Manor

His Scandalous Kiss

The Earl's Complete Surrender

Lady Sarah's Sinful Desires

At The Kingsborough Ball

The Danger in Tempting an Earl

The Scandal in Kissing an Heir

The Trouble with Being a Duke

The Summersbys

The Secret Life of Lady Lucinda

There's Something About Lady Mary

Lady Alexandra's Excellent Adventure

Standalone Titles

The Girl Who Stepped Into The Past

How Miss Rutherford Got Her Groove Back

Novellas

Diamonds in the Rough

The Roguish Baron

The Enterprising Scoundrels
Mr. Clarke's Deepest Desire

Mr. Donahue's Total Surrender

The Townsbridges
An Unexpected Temptation

A Duke for Miss Townsbridge

Falling for Mr. Townsbridge

Lady Abigail's Perfect Match

When Love Leads To Scandal

Once Upon a Townsbridge Story

The Honorable Scoundrels
The Duke Who Came To Town

The Earl Who Loved Her

The Governess Who Captured His Heart

Standalone Titles
Sealed with a Yuletide Kiss (An historical romance advent calendar)

The Secrets of Colchester Hall

Mistletoe Magic (from Five Golden Rings: A Christmas Collection)

Miss Compton's Christmas Romance

CHAPTER ONE

London, June 1817

S louched in his favorite armchair, Anthony Gibbs, Duke of Westcliffe, balanced a glass of brandy between his fingers while doing his best to ignore the problem hanging over his head. His good friends, Brody Evans, the Duke of Corwin, and Callum Davis, the Duke of Stratton, kept him company.

Anthony was grateful for it. There was no one else with whom he'd rather share his woes than these two men. They'd grown up together, had attended Eton together, and had even been together when the tragic news of their fathers' deaths had been delivered. Furthermore, they found themselves in similar straits and were able to relate.

The light from a nearby oil lamp illuminated Anthony's drink. He peered through the crystal, allowing the amber liquid to fracture his view of the parlor. If only he could sit here forever, snubbing life and the endless duties stacked on his shoulders. If only he could find the answers to his problems in the numerous glasses of brandy he'd been enjoying these past five hours.

If only...

"I need a solution," he muttered. Lord, he was tired. Perhaps he should tell his friends to go home so he could go find his bed.

"Don't we all?" Brody asked. He was stretched out on the floor, arms folded behind his head while he stared at the ceiling. His dark blonde hair was as rumpled as his clothes. "Finn's gambling addiction isn't helping with my financial predicament."

Finn was Brody's younger brother and he was forever getting himself into worse trouble than Brody, which was saying something.

"My concern is for Peter's future. His education will be costly." Callum pinched the bridge of his nose. "I don't know what my cousin was thinking when he and his wife made me their son's guardian."

"You're a duke," Anthony pointed out. "As such, they probably expected you to provide their son with endless possibilities."

Callum gave an unhappy laugh and went to refill his glass. His black hair was darker than Anthony's and made him look slightly dangerous in the dim lighting. "The poor boy won't have any unless I find a way to replenish the coffers. My investments haven't made the returns I'd hoped for."

"Neither have mine," said Brody. "Quite the opposite."

Anthony could only concur.

The truth was they were all in a terrible bind. Managing estates and securing their futures had not been their priorities when they inherited their titles. Shock and grief had strengthened their bond, but it had also made them reckless. Instead of embracing responsibility, they'd spent the last three years on roguish pursuits. The need to block out the pain of losing their fathers in that terrible accident had led to excessive spending and extreme negligence.

"Keeping up appearances is becoming a chore," Anthony said. When he'd descended to breakfast that morning, his secretary had handed him an unpleasant stack of bills. Apparently, several shops had chosen to revoke his line of credit and were now demanding immediate payment. "With my sisters' debuts next season, it's time for me to stop being so damn irresponsible. I've got to do better. For their sakes."

Hell, even White's was threatening to cancel all of their memberships, which was why they'd gathered at Anthony's home for a change. So they wouldn't have to face the embarrassment of being publicly reminded of their outstanding payments.

If they weren't careful, their servants would quit and they'd have to cook their own meals.

"What do you have in mind?" Brody asked. He sat up and flung one arm loosely over his bent knee.

Anthony set his glass on the small round table beside his chair. "We're all in desperate need of incomes. So let's try to find a solution. There must be some way for us to cover our expenses, some means by which to resolve our financial problems and start making a profit."

"How?" Callum asked. "As members of the peerage we have limited options. We were our fathers' heirs and as such, we were never expected to seek employment as barristers, solicitors, or members of the clergy. We have no useful skills."

"True." Brody reached for the bottle of wine he'd left on the floor nearby and sighed when he found it empty. A vacant pause followed before he told his friends, "We could marry."

"What?" Anthony and Callum spoke in unison, their voices equally strained.

Brody shrugged. "You have to admit that it would solve the problem."

The clock on the fireplace mantel decided to chime at that moment, the sound too reminiscent of wedding bells for Anthony's liking.

"I for one am not prepared to tie the matrimonial knot just yet," he said, already regretting the conversation he'd recently had with Viscount Ebberly. It made him feel sick just thinking about it.

"Nothing would compel me to spend the rest of my life shackled to any of the ladies currently available on the marriage mart." Callum raised his glass in salute and gulped down a decent measure. "Least of all Miss Amanda Starling. Good lord. Can you imagine?"

The comment forced additional queasiness through Anthony's veins. He didn't care for Viscount Ebberly's daughter at all, but during a moment of desperation, he'd still gone to speak with her father. His intention had merely been to discover whether or not Miss Starling might be willing to fill his coffers in exchange for a title. The answer to that had been a resounding yes.

Ebberly had even suggested they meet with his solicitor the very next day, which had caused an entirely different kind of panic to surge through Anthony. Apologizing profusely, he'd attempted to make a hasty retreat, insisting he'd merely been trying to weigh his options. Only to have the viscount suggest that he spend some time getting to know his daughter better. In exchange, she would befriend his sisters and help them prepare for their debuts.

The suggestion proved how shrewd Ebberly was.

He'd taken Anthony's measure and had concluded that such a bargain was too good for him to pass up. Ebberly hadn't been wrong, but he had severely misjudged Anthony if he believed the arrangement would lead to courtship and marriage.

Intent on helping his sisters while avoiding a life sentence with Miss Starling, Anthony had determined to make sure they were never completely alone. They could perhaps meet for tea at a public venue or walk in the park with others present. But then, much to his relief, nothing more had come of the conversation. He'd not heard from Ebberly since and had permitted himself to dismiss his concerns regarding Miss Starling.

"I'll admit it's not ideal," Brody said, breaking through Anthony's thoughts, "but a large dowry might be precisely what I need."

"I disagree. If anyone in your family ought to marry, it should be Finn." Anthony leaned forward and, resting his forearms on his thighs, met Brody's gaze. "He's deliberately making things worse for you, and as such, it makes sense for him to take the fall."

"Perhaps, but you know as well as I that it will take an impressive title to tempt a father into letting his daughter marry a man without a fortune. Finn is a second son and a renowned scoundrel with little besides his looks to commend him. He's the exact opposite of what one might consider eligible."

"True," Callum muttered. "The only sort of

woman who'd wed him is one with scandal attached to her name. And the last of those was snatched up by Baron Hastings last week."

A moment of silence followed as they proceeded to mourn the poor baron losing his freedom. Sadly, Hastings had been in a similar situation to Anthony and his friends and had chosen to walk the proverbial plank in order to prevent the loss of his properties.

"Unfortunately, I will have to sacrifice myself," Brody said. "And the two of you may have to do the same if you want what's best for those who depend upon you."

Anthony knew this to be true, but the thought still made him shudder. He shook his head. One way or another, he'd have to get out of the mess he'd gotten himself into. "Absolutely not. We'll find another way."

"I don't see how w—"

"Let's allow ourselves three days to think it over," he suggested, cutting Callum off. "During that time, we'll all do our best to come up with an alternate plan."

"And if we don't?" Brody asked, his voice weary and much too resigned for Anthony's liking.

"Then we may have to consider the unspeakable." Anthony looked at each of his friends. "But I forbid you from doing so until we're certain there's no other choice. Agreed?"

When Callum and Brody both nodded, Anthony smiled with every intention of giving them hope. Even though his own had already jumped off the edge of a cliff. Optimism was the only way forward. The alternative would only lead to additional glasses of brandy and unacceptable results.

The trouble was, he decided in the following days, that every idea he came up with required funding. Even trade, which he was not too proud to engage in if it would help him and his friends maintain their independence. But attempting to start a business without collateral would be a giant waste of everyone's time.

So far, cutting costs and selling off superfluous items seemed the most promising way forward. He'd made an inventory last night of all the belongings he could do without and had been pleasantly surprised by the estimated income they'd fetch. If he could find buyers quickly, the sum might be enough to sustain him and his sisters for the next year, provided they all curbed their spending.

But since this was only a temporary fix, he'd still require a more sustainable source of income.

He sighed as he strolled along Oxford Street, looking for inspiration in all the shop windows. His friends were due to arrive at his townhouse in less than four hours. All he could do was hope one of them had been more imaginative than he.

A futile endeavor, he reflected, his attention

drawn by a handsome top hat in a milliner's window. He dismissed the item and kept on walking, past a cobbler, a winery, and a paper supply shop where he briefly considered ordering a new letterhead.

No. He had to be frugal from now on. Whatever money he had left should be spent only on necessities.

He knit his brow at this thought while some carriages clattered by. An acquaintance of his tipped his hat as they passed each other on the pavement.

A flash of red hair up ahead made him stop so abruptly the man behind him muttered a curse before saying, "The least you could do is step aside."

"I apologize," Anthony told him, his gaze fixed upon the approaching woman, just to be sure he wasn't mistaken.

The man shoved his way past and then the crowd parted, allowing Anthony a glimpse of the woman's face. It belonged to none other than the one woman he wished to avoid – a woman whose wealth was only surpassed by her ambition – the very same woman whose father he'd been foolish enough to discuss potential wedding plans with. Miss Starling.

With a shudder, he darted down a narrow side street and broke into a run, not stopping until he'd rounded a few more corners. Lord help him, that was close! Panting lightly, he leaned against a wall and closed his eyes briefly. The clamor from Oxford

Street had dimmed, giving way to fainter sounds. A cat meowed and a child's bright laughter drifted toward him. The slow clip-clop of a draught horse echoed from somewhere nearby.

Anthony pushed himself away from the wall and shoved his hands in his pockets. If only he'd listened to his secretary. Mr. Oats had warned him. Repeatedly. But Anthony had dismissed the man's concerns. He'd been a duke after all, with the world at his feet.

"Young and foolish, that's what you've been," he told himself with a snort of disgust. "An embarrassment to Papa's legacy."

Disheartened, he kept walking, making his way toward his home at Number 2 Berkley Square. A sign up ahead announced the presence of a bakery. After that, came a book shop. Between the Pages was its name.

Anthony stopped to look through the window where an assortment of books, some bound in leather and fabric, had been placed on display. The rest of the books, which remained unbound, were tilted against larger stacks to show off their titles. *Frankenstein* was among them – a novel Anthony had been avoiding because the subject didn't appeal.

Next to it, of far greater interest, was *Rob Roy*. He'd not yet purchased a copy, and though he knew he ought to be saving his money, he couldn't resist the distraction the book promised.

An older man with thick brown hair streaked with gray exited the shop. He carried a parcel under one arm and was turning back toward the still-open shop door when he spotted Anthony. Abandoning the door, he allowed it to swing shut before touching the brim of his hat. Interest lit up his eyes and he suddenly smiled.

"Good afternoon to you, sir," he said with good cheer. "Something catch your interest?"

Anthony chuckled. "Possibly. I was considering *Rob Roy*."

"An excellent choice. I dare say you won't find it cheaper anywhere else." He patted the parcel under his arm. "This shop delivers quality goods, excellent service, and very competitive pricing. If you've the time to spare, I recommend taking a closer look."

"Thank you. I just might do so."

The man responded with a satisfied nod and took his leave. Anthony watched him go before returning his gaze to the shop window. He laughed softly beneath his breath. What a curious encounter. If what the man had said was true though, the shop did warrant a closer look.

With his mind made up, Anthony pulled open the door and entered. A small bell above the entrance made a delightful tinkling sound to announce his presence. An understated smell of dust and paper greeted him, inviting him into a cozy interior. Several bookcases stood to Anthony's left and right filling the space, while a small wooden counter stood directly across from the entrance.

There were no other customers present, but the sharp sound of a gasp informed him he wasn't alone.

"Good afternoon?" He stepped forward and caught a glimpse of movement out of the corner of his eye. "I'd like to purchase a book."

A rustling sound followed but still no one appeared. Baffled, he rounded the first bookcase and tilted his head when he spotted what looked like a woman's body partially concealed behind the books on the next set of shelves. The top of her head was clearly visible, however. As were her shoes.

Anthony smiled and removed a book, creating a gap that allowed him to stare back into the clearest pair of blue eyes he'd ever beheld.

CHAPTER TWO

Heat rushed to Ada's cheeks. She squeezed her eyes shut and prayed for immediate invisibility.

"I can see you," a gentle voice rumbled. "Closing your eyes won't change that."

Ada cautiously peeked at the man staring back at her from the opposite side of the bookcase.

His eyes were a warm shade of gray, a remarkable color she'd not seen before. Fringed by thick, sooty lashes, they told a story of fun and mischief while also containing a vast degree of sadness around the edges.

They enchanted her, inspired her imagination, left her breathless and…

"Oompf!"

"Good lord." The stranger rounded the bookcase. "Are you all right?"

"No," Ada squeaked. Getting hit in the head with a book hurt like blazes.

Dropping her gaze, she stared at the offending tome which had toppled from the top shelf. She'd been trying to grab it, had almost managed to pull it free with the tips of her fingers, when the bell had chimed and she'd yanked her hand back while sucking in a sharp breath.

No one was meant to be here. Her uncle had told her he'd lock the door and put the 'Be Back Soon' sign in the window when he'd gone to deliver a special order to one of their oldest clients.

A movement immediately beyond the brick-sized book she'd been struck by drew her attention to a pair of gentlemen's boots. Black and polished to a high sheen, they informed her the wearer was someone of means.

Her gaze slid higher, over the top edge of the boots and up along muscular thighs wrapped in snug fawn-colored breeches. Ada's heart raced. Next came a pair of hands dressed in brown leather gloves, followed by a trim waist and firm chest encased in a deep shade of sapphire blue wool. A black silk waistcoat was worn underneath the jacket, along with a snowy white shirt.

Ada swallowed as she observed the wide shoulders and the beautifully styled cravat adorning the neck. The heat in her cheeks increased when she noted the angular jaw, the sensuous mouth set in a serious line, a straight nose, and those incredible eyes.

They were studying her from beneath dipped brows. Creases marred the man's forehead, but that did not deter from his dashing appearance. He was exceedingly handsome. Precisely as she imagined Mr. Darcy to look if he stepped from the pages of her favorite novel.

She sighed. Her knees grew weak and she sagged a little.

Strong hands caught her upper arms and then she was being maneuvered, turned about and steered toward a stool her uncle kept on the opposite side of the counter.

"Please sit," the stranger instructed, his low voice encouraging Ada to dutifully do so without any protest. Not that she'd any intention to. "I never considered a book shop a hazardous place, but my position on that has certainly changed. That was quite the blow you received and it shows. You're bleeding."

"Am I?" She raised her hand, prepared to feel for the wound, but he halted her movement.

"Allow me." He pulled his gloves off with his teeth, tossed them on the counter, and retrieved a handkerchief from his pocket.

Ada's stomach fluttered as anticipation raced through her. He stepped a bit closer, his thigh touching hers, and she became aware of his scent —

an inviting aroma that brought to mind cool country air and lemonade drinks on hot summer days. It was wonderfully fresh in the otherwise stuffy shop, but before she was able to savor it too long, he disrupted her thoughts with his ouch.

It was light and gentle, barely noticeable at all. But that didn't stop her pulse from leaping with very keen awareness. He dabbed at her, wiping a little here and there while angling her head to one side.

"Looks like a paper cut," he murmured while pressing his handkerchief to her brow. "Darn unlucky, I'd say."

Ada said nothing. She couldn't. Of all the ways in which she'd imagined her afternoon going, sitting here while some gorgeous stranger tended to her would not have occurred to her in a million years.

Not only because she avoided the shop during opening hours, but because she'd lived her entire life thus far without being noticed by any man. Least of all one as young and attractive as her would be rescuer.

She was her father's youngest daughter and as such her dreams of love and marriage were limited to the stories she read. Her dowry might have been larger had her father still lived. Unfortunately, he'd died when Ada was twelve, before he'd managed to make the same provisions for her as he'd made for his two eldest daughters.

Which was fine. Ada actually liked the education she'd gained from her uncle. He'd taught her how to bind books and how to neatly emboss the covers.

She was content and happy helping him with his small business. It was the least she could do to repay the kindness he'd shown toward her. And considering the trouble he seemed to be having these days with his increasingly stiff joints, she was reluctant to leave.

Her gaze darted toward the door and a new concern began manifesting. How could he have forgotten to lock it?

"Miss?"

Ada blinked. Her attention snapped back to the stranger. "Yes?"

The edge of his mouth lifted with a hint of amusement. "If you keep a bit of pressure on the handkerchief, your wound will soon stop bleeding."

Momentarily confused, she stared at him until he raised an inquisitive brow. "Oh. Right. Of course."

Heavens, he must think she'd hit her head harder than what was the case.

Straightening in an attempt to conceal her flustered state, she raised her hand so she could take over from him. Their fingers brushed during the brief exchange, and it was as though she'd touched a hot kettle. She gasped and went utterly still.

If he noticed, he gave no indication. Instead, he stepped away and glanced around the shop before turning to face her once more. "I don't suppose you know where the clerk might be?"

"Um…"

He returned to the spot where she'd stood when he'd first arrived and bent to pick up the fallen book. "*Soldier of Fortune* by Thomas Ashe. An interesting choice."

Ada shrugged. "It's one of the few novels I've not yet read."

CHAPTER THREE

Anthony gaped at the young woman who sat behind the counter. A tendril of dark blonde hair had come loose from her coiffure to curl across her shoulder. Dressed in a simple gown cut from light green fabric, she might have struck him as plain had her eyes not been the first thing he'd noticed about her.

But the blueness of her gaze had arrested him and forced him to pay attention as soon as he'd gotten a better look.

In doing so, he'd noticed her delicate features comprised of high cheekbones, a slim nose, a softly curved upper lip, and an elegant neck. She'd been staring at the floor, at the book that had landed upon her head. Until she'd realized he'd rounded the bookcase and was standing beside her.

Her gaze had shifted, travelling the length of his

body and causing his pulse to quicken. She'd raised her chin and his stomach had clenched when he'd spotted the blood on her brow. For reasons he could not explain, something about her – an innocent vulnerability he'd never encountered before – made him revolt against any harm coming to her.

Anthony dropped his gaze to the book in his hand and dismissed the notion. How ridiculous of him to have such musings about an absolute stranger.

"You've read the rest?" he asked when he became aware of the silence between them.

"With a few exceptions. *Frankenstein* and *The Vampyre* don't appeal to me much, and there are some other works I've attempted without completing."

"Your library must be impressive."

She bit her lip, appeared to consider how best to respond, and finally sighed. "I live upstairs. My uncle owns the shop."

"Really?" Not a Society miss then but someone whose story held much more interest.

"He said he'd lock up when he went to run a quick errand, so I thought I'd be able to grab a new book without being seen."

This got his attention. "You do not wish to be seen?"

"I do not wish to have my presence here questioned." She dropped her gaze and knit her brow.

"My uncle has been good to me. It would pain me if I were to damage his reputation."

Intrigued, Anthony approached the counter and placed *Soldier of Fortune* upon it. Thumbing through the first pages, he casually asked, "How would you do that?"

"Surely you can imagine." When he said nothing, she explained, "Many believe books can threaten the vulnerable mind of any woman. Especially when the woman in question is able to read what she wishes without a father or husband to guide her. As is my case."

"I don't subscribe to that notion."

"Then you are more progressive than most." Shifting her weight on the stool, she pulled her hand away and studied the handkerchief. "Am I still bleeding?"

"No. It appears the bleeding has stopped."

"Then I should return this to you. My apologies for having ruined it." She folded the handkerchief and held it toward him.

Anthony took it and tried to figure out how to continue their conversation. For some peculiar reason, he was reluctant to leave. There was still time to spare before his meeting and besides, he'd yet to purchase his book. Ah yes! "*Frankenstein* and *The Vampyre* have not tempted me either. I came in here hoping to purchase *Rob Roy*."

"An enjoyable read which I'm sure you'll like. I'll fetch it for you."

She slid off the stool, rounded the counter, and hurried past Anthony, disappearing between two bookcases. When she returned, she carried three books of which only one had been bound. She gave him a hesitant look before placing them on the counter and pushing the leather-bound book toward him.

"If you're eager to start reading today, you can purchase this copy of volume one now and have volume two delivered later this evening. If you desire a different color leather, however, I'm afraid you'll have to wait until tomorrow."

Anthony considered his options. Although he looked forward to relaxing with a new book, he also enjoyed chatting with this intriguing young woman. He wanted to see her again, he realized, and picking up books would serve as a subtle excuse.

"Blue would be my preferred choice," he murmured, finding her gaze and succeeding to hold it for one long second. Until color rose to her cheeks and she lowered her chin.

She swallowed and started arranging the books in a neat pile on top of the counter. "I'll…um…yes. We have a few shades to choose from, though I really should let my uncle handle your order."

"I won't tell a soul you helped me," Anthony promised.

Uncertainty knit her brow and pushed her lips into a flat line. She hesitated, then nibbled her lower lip. Eventually, she huffed a breath. "Very well."

Victory was his. He could have hooted with joy but limited himself to rocking back on his heels. How perfectly silly of him to be thrilled by winning this woman's agreement. He scratched the nape of his neck while she brought the samples of blue leather for him to consider. It took him only a moment to locate the right one, after which she collected a notepad and started to write.

"Name?" she inquired.

Sensing his title might make things awkward, he made a split-second decision. "Gibbs. And you are?"

"Miss Quinn," she informed him stiffly while scribbling away with frantic movements. "I'll need your address for the delivery, Mr. Gibbs."

"No need." When she stilled, he told her, "I'll stop by personally to pick up my order tomorrow afternoon at the hour best suited to you."

"Oh…I…um…"

"What's your favorite novel, Miss Quinn?"

Her lips parted. "What?"

Congratulating himself for having directed her attention away from what his comment suggested, he smiled in response to her obvious confusion. It wouldn't do for her to get all worked up and nervous over him wanting to see her again. For although she was quite adorable in her current state of being, he feared she'd go back into hiding if he made her too self-aware.

"You've clearly read a lot. More than I or anyone of my acquaintance, I'll wager. So tell me, if you knew you'd be stranded on a desert island with no other company than one novel, which would you choose?"

"*Pride and Prejudice.*"

Her answer was instantaneous.

Anthony tilted his head. "I've never heard of it. What's it about?"

The pink color in her cheeks deepened until she'd turned scarlet. "The meeting and subsequent courtship between a gentleman and a lady."

"A romance?"

She cleared her throat. "Yes."

"I don't understand." It sounded as dull as watching paint dry. "You'd rather be stuck with such a book than one that's filled with adventure and intrigue?"

"Adventure comes in all shapes and forms. In *Pride and Prejudice* it's emotional in nature, and the intrigue is not in short supply either."

"Hmm…"

She raised her chin and for the first time since they'd met, he saw a determined gleam in her eyes. "You're not convinced."

"Not really. Was it popular?"

"The copies my uncle ordered sold out within the

first month of publication. The articles I read in the paper a few years ago when the book was released confirmed it to be a massive success. So much so a second edition was printed later that very same year."

Enthralled by the passion with which she spoke, he leaned toward her. "Why do you love it so much?"

The edge of her mouth lifted, producing the most enchanting dimple he'd ever seen. "It's witty and clever, and although the characters have their flaws, they grow through their interactions with one another, becoming better versions of themselves in the process. Yes, the hero is arrogant to begin with and the heroine far too ready to judge him unfairly, but as the story unfolds, they acknowledge their mistakes, overcome their differences, and live happily ever after."

"Unless you're about to tell me there's a battle somewhere in the middle, I think I'll stick with *Rob Roy* and other works of that nature."

"Of course there's a battle, but it pertains to human nature, not to a military campaign or a brawl. But there *is* a scandal involving a dastardly rogue."

Finally something that might compel him to give the novel a chance if he had nothing else to read. "Who's the author?"

"Her name has only recently been revealed as

Jane Austen. She's also written *Sense and Sensibility, Mansfield Park, Em—*"

"*Mansfield Park* sounds familiar." He tried to recall where he'd head that title before. "I believe one of my sisters may have read it."

"You have sisters?"

He grinned. "You needn't sound so surprised. Yes. I have two. Twins, actually, though not identical in the least. They're sixteen years of age."

"Ready for their debuts," she murmured, a distant look in her eyes.

Provided he could afford the expense. He shook his head. There was no avoiding his duty. Somehow, he'd have to scrape the funds together. As regrettable as it was, he had no choice but to part with some of his assets. He'd already determined that his horses would help him pay the most immediate bills. And if he sold only one at a time, it was unlikely anyone would take much notice.

"These should be ready for you by three o'clock tomorrow afternoon," Miss Quinn said. "I realize this is irregular but we don't accept credit, so you'll have to pay up front when you come to collect the books. One pound, four shillings will be your total."

Anthony glanced at the note where she'd boldly written the sum he owed. He nodded and slipped it into his pocket. The time had come for him to leave. His friends would be arriving soon. "It's been a pleasure, Miss Quinn. I look forward to seeing you again."

A shy smile graced her lips, accentuating her beauty. "Don't be too quick to dismiss Miss Austen's books, Mr. Gibbs. They sold exceedingly well and probably earned her a small fortune."

Anthony stilled. "Did it perchance outdo *The Corsair?*"

"Probably not. That book beat every record. But the appeal of Miss Austen's novels and her unfortunate death last year does leave a gap in the market. As sad as it may be, it's a wonderful opportunity for an aspiring romance author. Competing against the likes of Byron or Sir Walter Scott would be next to impossible."

He blinked a few times while that piece of information sank in. "You don't say."

"It's certainly something worth keeping in mind. Don't you think?"

"Indeed I do." He smiled at her, bid her a lovely evening, and departed with the thrill of possibility propelling him forward.

CHAPTER FOUR

Ada waited for the shop door to swing shut behind Mr. Gibbs. As soon as it did, she expelled the deep breath she felt as though she'd been holding since his arrival. Goodness gracious, the poor man must think her daft with her prattling on the way she'd done. She could scarcely recall what she'd said. Or what *he'd* said for that matter. All she'd known was him and his rather breathtaking presence.

Nitwit.

She dropped her gaze and stared at the note she'd prepared. Her heart beat a bit faster with the reminder that he would return. Tomorrow, he'd said. Or was she the one who'd suggested the time?

The bell above the door chimed and Ada looked up to find Uncle James walking happily toward her. She narrowed her gaze. "Where have you been?"

He grinned. "You know the answer to that, Ada."

"Of course." She crossed her arms and uncrossed them again, placing both hands on her hips. "You didn't lock up when you left."

"Didn't I?" He sent the door an incredulous glance. "Must have slipped my mind. Sorry about that. Is the tea ready?"

"No. I'm sorry. We had a customer. A gentleman wanting to purchase *Rob Roy*. So I didn't manage to make the tea yet." With jerky movements, she gathered the leather samples she'd used and flashed a smile. "I'll do so right now."

"What was he like?" Uncle James inquired, following her to the back room where the books on order were bound. It narrowed toward a small rear entrance where a steep flight of stairs led to the upstairs apartment. A range comprising a compact oven and boiler was squeezed into the corner next to the back door.

"Talkative," she said, deliberately avoiding words like impressive and remarkable while grabbing a ladle. "Unfamiliar with Jane Austen's work."

"I take it you tried to win him over?"

Ada chuckled and proceeded to scoop some hot water into a teapot. "If I could convince you, I daresay there's hope for all men."

"And?" Uncle James leaned against the doorjamb and watched Ada swirl the water to heat the pot, then pour it out before adding fragrant dry leaves from a canister. "Did you make a sale?"

She rubbed the back of her neck and filled the pot with fresh hot water. "Yes. He will return tomorrow afternoon to collect his books. They're to be bound in blue leather."

"Ah. So you'll see him again."

Ada turned to face her uncle more fully. "I shouldn't. As it is, I ought to have turned him away."

"Why didn't you?"

Because she'd been awestruck by his eyes.

"A book fell on my head and I got distracted."

"Really?"

"It's not funny," Ada insisted, noting the way his lips twitched and doing her best not to laugh as well. "We were alone together for quite some time. It was completely inappropriate. If someone had seen…"

Uncle James appeared to mull that over while she collected two cups from the cupboard. "Did anyone see?"

"No. But that doesn't change the fact that I am a young, unmarried woman." She poured the tea. "I shouldn't be working in a bookshop to begin with, never mind dealing with young men like Mr. Gibbs unless there's a chaperone present."

"You're right. I apologize. It won't happen again." Uncle James accepted the cup she handed to him. "When Mr. Gibbs returns tomorrow, I'll meet with him while you remain hidden away in here as usual."

Ada's gut twisted. Despite her protestations, she wasn't sure she liked the sound of that. "There's a chance he'll ask for me."

"I suppose so, but I can always tell him you've gone out."

"Hmm…" She was starting to see the wisdom in thinking before speaking. Setting her cup to her lips, she sipped her tea. "If you're there, I believe it ought to be fine."

"Yes." Uncle James nodded. "I suppose you're right about that."

Happy to have steered things back in the right direction, Ada sent him a warm smile. "Now that's settled, I probably ought to start on the binding."

"In that case, I'll prepare a list of upcoming releases to order and update the ledger." He returned to the shop, but before closing the door he told her softly, "Every Elizabeth Bennett belongs with her own Mr. Darcy, Ada. Even you."

She spun toward him so she could question his meaning, but the door was already shut. Rather than yank it open and ask for an explanation, she simply stood there, staring. At nineteen years of age she ought to set her sights on marriage, but to pin her hopes and dreams on the likes of Mr. Gibbs, whose waistcoat probably cost more than her entire wardrobe, would be as pointless as wishing upon a star.

He belonged to a different world – one that

would be as impossible for her to enter as it would be for her to step into one of her novels. But she would see him tomorrow. Briefly. After which she'd return to solid ground and accept the hand she'd been dealt.

It did not escape Anthony's notice that his friends were gaping at him as though he'd sprouted horns.

"You want us to what?" Brody asked, the biscuit he'd been about to bite into seemingly forgotten.

"I realize the notion of writing a love story might be unpleasant, but please hear me out before you dismiss it entirely." They were gathered in Anthony's parlor once more, this time around the sofa table where three large plates filled with biscuits, cake, and sandwiches, had been placed for them to enjoy.

Stalling for a moment, Anthony topped up his coffee and took a quick sip. "From what I gather, Miss Austen's books were very popular. They sold exceedingly well. And no current author provides the sort of stories she wrote."

"Ones destined to fill women's heads with nonsense?" Callum snorted. "Romance is the last thing anyone ought to consider when contemplating marriage."

"I'll grant you that convenience should factor in – that one should not be dismissive of class and upbringing or of the wealth each party provides." Dropping his gaze, Anthony stared into his coffee while trying to marshal his thoughts. Miss Quinn was not of his class, yet he could not forget her or the connection he'd felt with her during their brief encounter. She'd...marked him, somehow. Glancing back up, he saw his friends' curious gazes as they waited for him to say something more. He cleared his throat. "I think most people want more than that though. Personally, I'd want to marry a woman I like spending time with. Not just—"

"Hold on." Brody was shaking his head. "Yesterday when we spoke, you were opposed to marriage."

"Because the only incentive was money. But what if it didn't have to be? What if we could marry for love or, at the very least, write about doing so?" He shifted his gaze between Brody and Callum. "People read novels in order to travel to faraway places, to go on adventures, to escape the drudgery of their everyday lives. And apparently there's good money in it – enough, I believe, to get the three of us out of the trouble we're in."

"I don't know," Callum said. "Writing a novel will take a long time. I can't wait years to earn an income, Anthony. I need funds now."

"We all do," Anthony agreed. "And I'll admit that does pose a problem, though I have begun considering measures that I believe you'll also benefit from."

"Such as?" Brody finally took a bite of his biscuit. The caution with which he'd posed the question conveyed his fear of potential drawbacks.

"Although we may be short on currency, we've all got plenty of costly possessions." Anthony cleared his throat. "I would suggest we liquidate a few in order to cover our current expenses. Just enough for us to get by from month to month until we've published our novel and started earning an income."

"I don't know," Callum muttered. "We're dukes with reputations to uphold. Our situation is embarrassing enough without it becoming public knowledge."

"Agreed," Brody said, "though Anthony does have a point. We're living beyond our means. It's actually quite ridiculous, how incapable we are of settling our debts. On paper, we're all extremely wealthy, yet here we are, reduced to meeting at each other's homes because we can't afford going out."

Callum nodded. "I suppose you're right."

"I'm already arranging to sell one of my horses," Anthony told them. "I've got six, which is more than I actually need, and the income will go a long way to helping my sisters prepare for their Season. They are my priority now. If I can ensure their futures, I might just forgive myself for bungling this duke business."

"You were destroyed," Brody murmured. "We all were. Getting over that kind of loss at an age when we depended upon our fathers to show us the way was rough on us all."

This was true. The impact of the news they'd received had been crippling. But they hadn't been children. As such, they should have been wiser. "The situation we faced does not excuse our stupidity."

"You're right," Callum said. Leaning forward, he braced his forearms on his thighs and met Anthony's gaze directly. "How long do you suppose it would take us to write this book you have in mind and get it published?"

"Hold on." Brody stared at Callum, his eyes wide with surprise. "You're not actually considering this idea are you?"

"Why not?" Callum transferred a piece of cake to his plate and stabbed it with his fork, scattering crumbs on the table. "I haven't been able to think of a way for us to make money without either seeking employment or taking a chance at the races. Have you?"

Brody frowned. "No, but a love story? Really? Could we not write something like *Treasure Island*, *Gulliver's Travels*, or *Don Quixote* instead?"

"Doing so would require extreme originality and a tremendous marketing effort. It would involve competing against the likes of Sir Walter Scott." Anthony added a bit more milk to his coffee. "He has published a book every year since *Waverly*'s debut in 1814, which means he'll soon be releasing another. So I say it's better for us to write something different – something readers are currently missing – a novel intended to fit a vacant slot."

Brody snorted. "As much as I'd like to argue, you make a compelling point. How the devil did you come up with all this?"

"I, er…met someone." Anthony deliberately picked up his cup and proceeded to drink.

"Who?" Callum asked just before popping a piece of his cake in his mouth.

Anthony hesitated. He wasn't quite ready to share his encounter with the delightful Miss Quinn. Or, more to the point, have his friends tease him about it. As they would likely do.

"A bookshop clerk." Deciding to move on swiftly, he said, "Look, I realize it's a bit of a challenge, but I do think we can get the job done if we work together. You asked about time, Callum. If we go about this the right way, it shouldn't take more than a couple of weeks to write the first draft."

"You're thinking we'll all write at the same time?" Brody asked.

"Precisely. Thirty pages per day between the three of us. Beginning, middle, and end. We'll stitch everything together once we're finished and smooth out the transitions."

Callum straightened. "Has such a thing ever been done before?"

Anthony shrugged. "I've no idea, but it does seem like the most efficient way forward."

"It's certainly an interesting challenge," Brody muttered with more excitement than he'd shown thus far. "How do we begin?"

Anthony stood and went to collect some blank sheets of paper and a pencil. "By coming up with an interesting plot, I should think."

CHAPTER FIVE

Excitement swirled in Ada's stomach as soon as she woke the next morning. She tried to enjoy her breakfast, but found it hard to sit still. Today, she would see Mr. Gibbs again, perhaps for the very last time since his business with Between the Pages would be completed. He'd have no reason to stop by again. Unless he chose to. Which she supposed he might since he did like to read and might need a new book once he finished the one he was buying today and–

Oh, why was she getting wound up over this? He was just another customer.

A handsome one, to be sure, and one who'd happened to help her too. But it was ludicrous of her to make more of their brief encounter than that. It was certainly irrational of her to let his impending visit tangle her nerves.

"Is something the matter?" Uncle James inquired.

"Why do you ask?"

"Because we're having kipfels and you always eat them with gusto, except you've barely eaten more than two bites this morning."

Ada looked at her crescent shaped pastry, fresh from the bakery next door. She'd sliced it open and buttered the inside, just as she liked it. "I'm afraid I don't have much appetite today."

"Oh?"

"There's still the embossing to be done on Mr. Gibbs's order."

"I thought you finished it yesterday." Uncle James's spoon clinked against his teacup as he added sugar and stirred. "It doesn't usually take you this long to complete a binding."

Ada groaned and sent him a helpless smile. "I couldn't decide whether to make the spine simple or decorative. The floral motifs I designed would look pretty against the blue background, but what if he thinks it too feminine?"

Uncle James sipped his tea. "I believe Mr. Gibbs will appreciate a personal touch. Use the stamps you've designed, Ada."

For some peculiar reason, doing so caused her heart to beat faster. She nodded and took another bite of her kipfel before excusing herself from the table. "I'd best get on with it then. The gold paint needs time to dry, and it's already nearing eight o'clock."

Leaving her uncle to finish his breakfast, she descended the stairs to the storage room and crossed to the heavy worktable she used. The books she'd bound the previous day were neatly positioned side by side. Ada checked the volumes to make sure they were ordered correctly then searched her collection of stamps until she found the right ones.

She opened the cover of the first book and placed it over a wooden block before cleaning the surface with a damp cloth. Using a ruler as a spacer, she heated the first stamp, positioned it, and gave it a few sharp hits with a hammer before checking the imprint. A lovely border had appeared with floral arrangements in each of the corners. They were joined by thin lines running the length of each side.

Satisfied, Ada repeated the stamping for the back of the book as well as for the other volume before stamping the spine with floral imprints to match. Once this was completed she went to work preparing the titles, complete with volume number and author name. Letters were carefully positioned in a tray and locked into place before being correctly aligned and stamped, both on the front and on the spine.

"How's it coming along?" Uncle James inquired when he came downstairs.

Ada looked up from the bowl she'd just filled

with some egg whites she meant to use as adhesive glair. She grabbed a brush. "Very well, thank you."

"I'll leave you to it then, shall I?" He unlocked the door leading into the shop and stepped through it, pausing only briefly to wish her good luck before shutting the door behind him.

Alone again, Ada painted on the glair with swift strokes then left it to dry while preparing the gold leaf.

She straightened briefly to rotate her shoulders and stretch her arms before bowing over the table once more. Moving with practiced ease, she laid the gold leaf over the areas she had prepared and brushed it with oil to secure it. Lining up the stamps she'd initially used with the marks already made, she took a deep breath and impressed the gold into those areas.

Please be perfect.

It was funny, in a way, how she always dreaded mistakes no matter how many times she completed a binding. But she prided herself on perfection – on completing exceptional work – and did not want to discover an offset between the initial indentation and the subsequent one, or a variance in the gold. Unable to accept such a thing or deliver it to a paying customer, she'd have to start over.

Lifting her hand, she removed the stamp and set it aside so she could brush the excess gold away. So far, so good. She expelled a slow breath and continued her work, imprinting the rest of the gold until she'd completed her task. A light dusting of French chalk was added to help remove the residue from the oil, and this was then wiped away with a clean cloth.

Ada took a slow breath and expelled it. Her lips quirked and she finally smiled.

Perfect.

The door to the shop opened and Uncle James popped his head into the room. "Are you almost finished?"

"Yes." Ada stood and stepped back from the table so she could admire her work properly. "It's all done."

"Good." He glanced at the books. "Those look beautiful, Ada. I dare say it's some of your finest work yet. But I want you to eat. That's why I came. To let you know it's already noon."

"Is it?" Ada glanced at the clock behind her. "Heavens, time certainly knows how to fly. Shall I bring some food down from upstairs so we can eat here?"

"How about we purchase a couple of mutton pies from next door instead?"

Ada grinned in response to the hopeful look in her uncle's eyes. It was no secret that neither of them was a good cook, and whatever she offered to make would be boring at best, inedible at worst. She nodded. "An excellent suggestion. I'll go and purchase them right away."

It was convenient having a bakery next door, though possibly detrimental to one's figure in the long term, Ada mused as she paid for the fresh pies. The paper in which they were packed was warm to the touch, and the scent filling her nostrils made her eager to taste the food.

She handed one to Uncle James as soon as she returned to the shop. Since they were the only two people present, they chose to eat at the counter instead of retreating to the back room. Ada bit into her pie and savored the hearty chunks of tender meat that spilled from beneath the flaky crust.

Delicious.

She ate the entire thing in less than ten minutes and was just dusting crumbs from her fingers when the front door opened and Mr. Gibbs entered to the bell's happy chime. Ada took a sharp breath and slid off the stool on which she'd been sitting. Feeling incredibly stiff and awkward, she clutched her hands and tried to ignore the sudden onslaught of topsy-turviness in her stomach.

Impeccably dressed in a forest green jacket and slate gray trousers, Mr. Gibbs approached with a wide smile directed solely at her. "Good day, Miss Quinn. How delightful it is to see you again."

"Welcome back, Mr. Gibbs." Dear lord, she could

feel her cheeks starting to burn. Sensing a need for stability, she reached for the stool.

Mr. Gibbs's gaze slid toward her uncle. He tilted his head. "I say, aren't you the same fellow I met in the street yesterday, in front of this very shop?"

Ada's lips parted as she turned to stare at her uncle with no small amount of surprise.

He chuckled. "Afraid so. I hope you can forgive my cheekiness in recommending my own shop to you."

"An easy feat since your advertisement was correct. As far as I can tell so far, the shop does indeed deliver quality goods, excellent service, and very competitive pricing." Mr. Gibbs glanced at Ada and, holding her gaze, quietly added, "I'm certainly glad I decided to take a closer look."

The heat in her cheeks worsened until she felt as though she'd been engulfed by flames. Lord help her, this man had the power to melt her completely.

"I'll see about that box I started unpacking earlier." Uncle James sent Ada a pointed look accompanied by a knowing smile before wandering off and disappearing between a couple of bookcases.

Ada stared after him. This was the first she'd heard of a new delivery.

"Our conversation yesterday has given me much to consider," Mr. Gibbs said, drawing her attention back to him. "I've decided it would be unfair to judge something harshly without first examining it in greater detail."

"Oh?"

"I refer to Miss Austen's novels of course. You spoke of them with such fondness. Having never read one myself, I'll allow that my opinion of such books may have been overly rash."

Ada blinked. His ability to set aside his own preconceived notions was admirable. She smiled. "Thank you. I've always believed it important to keep an open mind in all matters."

The edge of his lips quirked with undeniable charm. "Quite. Which is why I thought to ask if the shop has a copy of your favorite book of hers. Pride and something or other, I believe you said."

"*Pride and Prejudice,*" Ada informed him with a chuckle. "Unfortunately, Miss Austen's books are so successful they sell out almost at once. If I'm not mistaken, there's still a copy of *Persuasion* left, but it's not as good. A bit too distressing for my own personal taste and lacking much of the clever wit that's prevalent in Austen's earlier works."

Biting her lip, she briefly considered lending Mr. Gibbs her personal copy of *Pride and Prejudice*, but quickly dismissed the idea. Such an offer was far too forward and would surely be viewed as an impropriety.

"Is it possible to place an order?" Mr. Gibbs

asked. "For the novels you think are among Miss Austen's best?"

Ada picked up a pencil and tapped the end of it lightly against the counter. "That would be four books in total. *Pride and Prejudice*, which you simply must read first, *Sense and Sensibility*, *Emma*, and *Mansfield Park*. If I recall correctly, you mentioned your sister having a copy of *Mansfield Park*, so maybe you don't need to purchase that one?"

"True." He was silent a moment before remarking, "Nevertheless, I'd like to have my own copy."

∽

Anthony waited quietly while Miss Quinn made a note of the titles. A light pink hue colored her cheeks, and despite displaying some shyness, she seemed more comfortable with him today. He was glad. Nervousness had never been a concern of his, yet there was no denying the worry holding his heart in a vice as he'd set out to fetch his order. He'd been afraid, truth was, that the strong connection he'd felt upon meeting Miss Quinn had been imagined.

But no. His concerns had been completely unfounded. The moment he'd entered the shop and his gaze had met hers, he'd known he was in the right place. The sparkle in her lovely blue eyes and her welcoming smile were proof that she had looked forward to seeing him just as much as he'd looked forward to seeing her.

"That will come to four pounds for the Austen books. We'll require a two-pound deposit, to be returned to you if we're unable to procure the books. And then there's *Rob Roy*. I'll fetch it for you straight away."

The total exceeded five pounds. More than what a skilled craftsman earned in a month. Enough to buy a cow. It was, without doubt, an enormous sum to spend on what most would consider an extravagant purchase. Especially for a man in his position.

Frivolous, Mama would say, but she wasn't here and besides, these weren't just books. They were research intended to help him make money.

Anthony watched Miss Quinn disappear into a back room. He wasn't ready to finish his dealings with her just yet, so when she returned, he casually said, "I hope you don't find this too intrusive, but I'm curious to know how you came to live here, above a bookshop."

She set his order on the counter. "My uncle used the money he inherited from his parents to open the place some twenty years ago. Considering how much books sell for, one might imagine him to be very well off. But after setting income aside for new books, paying the rent and other expenses, his own salary is modest. So he sold his townhouse ten years ago and moved into the space above the shop. When Papa died, Uncle James took me in."

"I'm sorry. I shouldn't have asked."

"It's all right. I could have refused to answer."

"Why didn't you?"

"I don't know, but there's something about you, I…" She shrugged and shook her head. "Confiding in you felt natural."

The warmth in his chest expanded. "I'm glad."

She chuckled, ducking her head with a hint of shyness. "I used to have my sisters to talk to, but they're older than I. Dorothy was already wed with Bethany just about to get married when our father died. She lives in Northumbria now and I… Heavens, why am I telling you all of this?"

He grinned. "Because I'm happy to hear what you have to say? My father died too a few years ago and Mama has since re-married. She and her new husband are currently traveling the world together."

"Sounds like you miss her."

"Yes. It's my fault she's gone. I pushed her away with my foolhardiness." He winced, a little embarrassed by the unplanned confession. Choosing to move on quickly, he said, "But I do have two younger sisters, both on the cusp of making debuts."

"How exciting."

Anthony managed a tight smile. Thankfully, both were provided with handsome dowries which he'd had no access to. But other expenses would be required if they were to make the desirable matches one might expect from a duke's sisters. There were, after all, reputations to uphold.

"I'm sure it is for them," he said as he gave his attention to the books she'd brought from the back room. He picked one up and turned it over, admiring the gold imprints upon the cover and along the length of the spine. "This is exquisite. The craftsmanship is extraordinary and this...this little ornamental symbol right here. I'm guessing it's a signature?"

"Yes...um...my uncle..." She waved her hand. "He's always believed in adding a binder's mark in order to–"

The shop door swung open behind him, and before Anthony had a chance to figure out what was occurring, Miss Quinn vanished behind a bookcase. Two older women entered and Miss Quinn's uncle came to assist them.

They also commented on the lovely editions he'd come to collect, and to Anthony's surprise, one of them said, "I did not think your rheumatism allowed you to keep on binding, Mr. Quinn. I'm relieved to see that's not the case. Indeed, this is some of your finest work to date."

"Thank you," Mr. Quinn murmured. He sent a quick glance toward the bookcase his niece was still hiding behind and proceeded to help the two women find what they wanted.

A purchase was made along with an order, and the pair soon departed with a polite, "Good day."

Anthony sent a quick look toward the bookcase. Leaning toward Mr. Quinn, he asked, his voice low, "How long has your niece been binding books for you?"

"I suppose it must be…" He stopped himself with a grin and tapped the side of his nose before retreating once more.

"Sorry," said Miss Quinn as she stepped back into view. With a hesitant glance directed toward the door, she moved back into position behind the counter. "Let's finish this order, shall we?"

"Have you ever considered letting customers know that you work here?" Anthony asked, leaning against the counter.

"I don't really," Miss Quinn informed him, her voice a bit edgy as she began wrapping his books.

"That's not the impression I'm getting," he murmured.

Her gaze shot toward his. "This is an irregularity. I… Please, you mustn't say a word. If it became known that an unmarried woman works here, the shop's reputation could be ruined. To say nothing about mine or my uncle's. Please, Mr. Gibbs, I hope you won't–"

"You needn't worry. I shan't tell a soul."

She expelled a visible sigh of relief, and he noted

her fingers trembled as she tied the string to hold the brown paper in place.

Regretting his comment and how anxious it clearly made her, he tried to think of something else to say – a subject to steer her attention elsewhere. An apology might do the trick.

He opened his mouth.

"I'll require an address for you along with the payment. So your books can be delivered when they arrive."

"Right." He retrieved the coins he owed and placed them on the counter. "I could just stop by and check from time to time."

She gave him an odd look. "I suppose so."

He flattened his mouth. She'd already shared a great deal about herself with him. Hiding his true self from her felt wrong. It wasn't the honorable way in which to start a new friendship.

"Number 2 Berkley Square," he said and watched as she jotted that down. When she finished, she added his name. Mr. Gibbs. Anthony took a deep breath. "There's a...ahem...slight error in need of correcting."

"Oh?" She stared at her note. "Forgive me, but I don't see it."

"It's the name."

"Ah. Just one 'b' rather than two? I'll just–"

He caught her hand to halt her movement and everything stilled, except the beat of his heart, which was thumping so hard he feared she might hear it. Her sharp intake of breath suggested she had.

He withdrew his hand slowly. "My name isn't exactly Mr. Gibbs. Not formally speaking. I... Promise me what I'm about to share won't change what's between us. I need to know that you won't perceive me differently."

She knit her brow. "That would honestly be an impossible promise to make without knowing what you've been hiding. But I've enjoyed our conversations so far and would like to believe nothing will influence that."

"The name should read, His Grace, the Duke of Westcliffe."

CHAPTER SIX

Three whole days had passed since Mr. Gibbs – the duke – had shocked Ada into silence. For several moments after his life-altering confession, she'd wondered if she'd been struck in the head by another book. She'd then proceeded to ponder the probability of two such occurrences happening to the same woman in the space of one week and hadn't realized her mouth had been hanging open until the duke asked if she was all right.

Embarrassment didn't begin to describe the emotional calamity she'd experienced. Riotous thoughts and feelings had stormed her brain as she'd struggled to regain her composure.

Not only because of who he was, but because of the tragedy that was attached to his title. She'd been dismayed when she'd read of it in the paper – three dukes, all simultaneously killed when they'd gone to purchase some livestock and a cow pen exploded.

Words had failed her when she'd realized she stood before one of these men's sons, frozen, with no idea how to respond.

Since their first encounter, she'd known *Mr. Gibbs* to be a man of elevated status. His attire, the gentlemanly air about him, and the way he moved, all attested to this. She'd known he stood apart from her sphere of existence.

And yet, in some strange way, a bridge had formed between her world and his. They'd chatted, laughed a little, gotten along. It had, she reflected, felt as though there might have been a chance for a deeper connection. A slim chance, perhaps, but a chance nonetheless.

Until he'd told her he was a duke.

Good lord. She might as well dream of wearing a gown made from stardust to the next ball. She felt like a fool. No, she *was* a fool. Allowing herself to hope a man of Mr. Gibbs's caliber would ever shower her with romantic attention was absolutely preposterous. Even while he'd been just Mr. Gibbs. Now that she knew him to be a duke, this line of pondering was downright mortifying.

"You're distracted today," Harriet said, prompting Ada to blink.

She'd come to the cozy space rented by the Earl of Rosemont's youngest daughter, Lady Emily

Brooke, for the monthly book club meeting she'd been attending this past year. The club was open to fellow enthusiasts and encouraged women from all social stations to join.

There were presently twenty members, including Emily's grandmother, the Viscountess Attersby, who was an absolute delight. Outspoken and energetic, the older woman would always fill her teacup with brandy before conveying her thoughts on the latest novel they'd all been assigned.

The meetings offered a lovely diversion from everyday life.

She glanced at her friend, aware she ought to say something. Unwilling to bring up Mr. Gibbs, she said, "I'm sorry. It's been a busy week at the shop."

"That's a good thing, isn't it?" Harriet asked, taking another sip of tea. Her curly red hair was unfashionably short, but the locks still had a charming effect, which was further enhanced by her forest green eyes.

"Certainly," Ada agreed. She bit her lip and watched as the other book club members began taking their leave. "How about you? Are you still working yourself to the bone or have you been able to get some more rest?"

"I'm here, aren't I?" Harriet shrugged. "My job doesn't allow for much rest, but I'll not complain about it, Ada. You know well enough that I love what I do and that I can't afford to risk losing the pay."

Following the deaths of both her parents, most recently her father, Harriet had been left to care for her significantly younger twelve-year-old sister, Lucy. Despite being born into gentry, neither Harriet nor her sister had been provided for in their father's will, since said will had been non-existent.

As a result, everything had gone to a rather detestable cousin who'd tossed them both out of their home immediately after the funeral. It was a blessing that Harriet had managed to find good employment, though Ada often wondered whether the lengths she'd been forced to in order to do so were worth it.

Ada glanced at Lucy, who always attended with Harriet. She was still playing with the marbles Emily kept here for her entertainment. "I believe it's a bit of a luxury to be fond of one's work."

"Having had jobs I hated, I have to agree," Harriet said, her voice quiet. She met Ada's gaze and smiled. "We're lucky, you and I, to get paid for something we enjoy doing."

Ada nodded. "We received several orders over the past few days, so my binding skills have been put to good use."

"I plan to order more books myself," Emily said as she came to join them after seeing her grand-mother out. Emily's fondness for books outdid her interest in men and marriage by leaps and strides. But what only a few select people knew was that

Emily also wrote a successful book review column for *The Mayfair Chronicle,* under the assumed name, The Lady Librarian.

"I look forward to it," Ada informed her. She loved it when either one of her friends stopped by the shop, since they'd often stay for a cup of tea and a lengthy chat.

"The last editions you prepared for me were absolutely stunning. I'm sure others will agree."

"They do," Ada said. She pursed her lips when she noted her friends' expectant gazes. "A lady remarked on my most recent work last week when she spotted the books on the counter."

"She must have been very pleased with her purchase," Harriet said.

"Oh, they weren't for her," Ada told them a bit too quickly. When both of her friends raised their eyebrows, Ada attempted a nonchalant shrug. "They were for a—" she cleared her throat "—gentleman."

"Really?" Emily's curiosity could not be denied. It was in the pointed look and that mischievous smirk she sent Ada. "Do I detect an interest on your part?"

"No." Not one that was worth entertaining. She decided to change the subject. "Have you given any more thought to your father's birthday gift?"

Emily nodded while munching a piece of short-bread she'd snatched from a plate. "There's a new edition of the *Encyclopædia Britannica.*"

"Yes, the fifth one," Ada said, recalling the two

complete sets that had just been delivered to the shop. "Consisting of twenty volumes."

"Right." Emily gulped down a mouthful of tea. "So I thought I'd give him that. It's a fairly large order requiring a lot of binding, so I hope you can find the time, Ada."

"Of course I can," Ada assured her. She reached for Emily's hand and gave it a light squeeze. "Thank you, by the way, for your constant mentions of Between the Pages in your column. I'm sure it has helped drive a lot of the traffic we've seen lately. Uncle James has certainly remarked on an increase in sales."

"It's my pleasure," Emily said. "That shop is a hidden gem that deserves to be discovered by anyone with an interest in books."

"I completely agree," Harriet said before glancing toward her sister. "Lucy, it's time to tidy up now so we can get going."

"Already?" Lucy asked.

"Unfortunately, yes. I'd like to catch Mrs. Newson before she closes her shop for the day." Harriet stood and shook out her coarse cotton skirts. She turned to Ada and Emily. "It was lovely seeing you both again."

"I'll walk with you," Ada said as she too rose to her feet.

"Take this." Emily handed Harriet a small bundle.

Harriet frowned at it. "Thank you, but you've

already done so much for me and Lucy. I really shouldn't be—"

"Nonsense," said Emily. "It's just a few things I don't use myself. Better it goes to a dear friend than to someone I don't know, as will happen if I let my maid dispose of the items."

Harriet sighed. "Very well then. Thank you, Emily. You're ever so kind."

Emily blushed slightly but waved her hand as though to dispel the effect Harriet's gratitude had upon her. She drew her and Ada into a simultaneous hug. "I'll miss you both until we see each other next."

"We'll miss you too," Ada assured her.

She and Harriet departed with Lucy in tow and exited onto Maypole Street. The smoke from newly lit fireplaces permeated the early evening air. Up ahead, coal was being shoveled into a chute.

"I'll see you next month," Harriet said when they parted ways at the next intersection.

"Looking forward to it," Ada said. She turned left while Harriet and Lucy headed toward the river, crossing the street behind a horse and cart.

The pavement Ada walked was freshly washed with the runoff water trickling along beside her. Lanterns would be lit in another hour or so. For now, the light from the sinking sun cast a wondrously hazy glow across the City.

She rounded a few more corners and was almost back at the bookshop when she spotted a man striding toward her from the opposite end of the street. Her heart seemed to recognize him before her eyes did, slamming so hard against her breast, it felt like she'd been hit by a shovel.

She halted for a brief second - just long enough to confirm that it was indeed him. The duke was back and her stomach had chosen this inopportune *time* to have a small seizure. Or at least that was how *it felt*.

He spotted her in the next instant and sent her the *sort* of dazzling smile that ought to be illegal. It certainly had the power to scatter all logical thought and weaken her knees, which was rather a frightening thing to consider. What if this was the general effect he had on everyone? Parts of London would come to a standstill, filled by mesmerized people all leaning up against buildings for support.

"Miss Quinn." He greeted her as though she were the sort of woman for whom an encounter with a duke was a normal occurrence. "I was just coming to see you."

"Ah…um…er…Your Grace?" She pushed one foot behind her and bent the front knee in an awkward attempt at a curtsey.

"I thought we agreed there'd be none of that." He dipped his eyebrows as though to show how serious he was, but the flicker of humor in his eyes betrayed him.

Ada sent him a hesitant smile. "Sorry. I'm just not used to this sort of thing."

"And what sort of thing might that be?"

"Socializing with someone as…" She swept her hand up and down as though painting him with an invisible brush.

His right eyebrow rose while the left side of his mouth drew upward to form a crooked grin. "Charming? Handsome? Likeable? Possibly all the above?"

She rolled her eyes but couldn't suppress a chuckle at his wry sense of humor. If he'd meant to put her at ease, it had the desired effect. She relaxed and approached, allowing her shoulder to playfully push against his as she turned for the bookshop door.

"Conceited does come to mind," she teased and promptly sent him a nervous look over her shoulder. "I'm sorry. That was perhaps a bit rude. I didn't mean to offend, I—"

"Stop." His grin had warmed his eyes, and he was watching her with the same sort of curious expression he'd worn while helping her when they'd first met. "I'm not some fragile glass ornament in danger of breaking if things get a little bit rowdy. On the contrary, I enjoy our repartee and would be devastated if you began tiptoeing around me just because of a silly title."

"Well, we can't have that," Ada said after a brief

pause. She took a deep breath and expelled it. "I enjoy our repartee too. It's surprisingly…"

"Easy," he murmured when she failed to come up with the right word.

"Yes," she agreed, a little surprised by how true this was.

She'd always struggled with friendships, finding it difficult to approach people. It had taken forever for her to pluck up the courage to attend the book club meeting the first time she'd gone. Uncle James had encouraged her to participate so she could meet other women her own age. She'd spent two hours just listening to everyone else. It wasn't until the meeting was over and she'd been about to leave that Emily stopped her to inquire about her reason for coming.

The next meeting had been easier and little by little she'd opened up.

In some ways, her friendship with Westcliffe was similar. He'd taken the lead by engaging her in conversation and encouraging her to participate. She was grateful to him for this. He was a wonderful man who wasn't entirely wrong about the adjectives he'd used to describe himself. But he could never be more than a friend.

Odd, how that thought sent a pang of regret through her heart.

She shook off the feeling and pushed open the shop door. The bell chimed and the wonderfully familiar scent of paper wrapped itself around her. Mr. Gibbs followed her inside. Perhaps she should start calling him Westcliffe? She'd have to ask him how he preferred she address him. Mr. Gibbs was how she thought of him, but it wasn't the right title for him anymore.

A customer stood at the counter – an older gentleman in the process of placing a new order with Uncle James. He glanced at Ada, whom he quickly dismissed, and then at Mr. Gibbs.

Recognition widened his eyes. "Your Grace. Do you shop here too?"

"Indeed I do," Mr. Gibbs informed him. "The service is excellent and I would dare any man to locate a more skillful binder."

"Agreed," said the gentleman while Ada snuck behind Mr. Gibbs and disappeared into the back room. "Mr. Quinn is the best there is."

"Yes," Ada heard Mr. Gibbs say with a pensive tone to his voice. "He most certainly is."

Ada waited until she heard the man leave before venturing back into the shop. "Would the two of you care for some tea?"

"I'd love a cup," Mr. Gibbs said. "If it's not too much of an imposition."

"Not at all," said Uncle James. "We're happy to have your company, aren't we, Ada?"

Heat rose to Ada's cheeks and she quickly nodded. "Of course."

She caught Mr. Gibbs's gaze briefly and swallowed before retreating to the back room once more, leaving him to chat with her uncle. With hasty movements intended to dispel the fluttery feeling in her stomach, she prepared the tea.

"You know him, you silly goose," she chided herself. "He's your friend. No sense in letting him ruffle your feathers."

If it were only so simple. Truth was, the man was able to make her skin tingle with merely one glance. It was equally wonderful and tormenting.

"We thought we'd join you in here," Uncle James said, showing Mr. Gibbs into the small space behind the shop. Ada, who was pouring hot water into the pot, started a bit in surprise, nearly scalding herself in the process. "It's a bit more private, in case other shoppers stop by."

"I suppose," Ada hedged, sweeping the area with her gaze and wondering how someone else might see it – how Mr. Gibbs, specifically, would see it. She set the pot aside and rushed to make space for him on a chair where she'd left leather samples scattered about in a messy pile. "I'm sorry. I wasn't expecting to entertain anyone."

Certainly not a duke. Good lord, whatever must he be thinking?

"No worries," he said, his voice cheerful as he inspected the room with a curious look. "I love how homely this feels. My townhouse seems so impersonal by comparison. Is this where you work, Mr. Quinn?"

Uncle James crossed to the wooden table Ada used for binding the books. "Oh yes. One doesn't need a large room for this sort of thing."

"Perhaps you can show me how it's done once we've finished our tea?" Mr. Gibbs sent Uncle James a warm smile. "I'm curious to see how it all comes together."

"Well...um...yes." Uncle James scratched the back of his head and glanced at Ada. "It's a bit of a lengthy process, though, with time required for drying the glair. But I can certainly walk you through the basics – explain how it's done, that is."

"Thank you. I'd enjoy that." Mr. Gibbs accepted the cup Ada handed him and gestured toward the chair she'd prepared for his use. "Why don't you sit here, Mr. Quinn, and I'll take one of the stools instead?"

"Oh no." Uncle James shook his head. "I couldn't possibly."

"Please." Mr. Gibbs remained where he stood. "I must insist."

"But you're a duke," Uncle James muttered. "It wouldn't be right."

Mr. Gibbs sighed. "Can we please agree that while I am here I am not any different from either of you? I'm not more deserving or of higher status. I am merely Mr. Gibbs, an ordinary man enjoying himself with his friends."

"Very well," Ada said before Uncle James could respond. The sincerity in Mr. Gibbs's voice, the quiet plea for them to treat him without any fuss, and the kindness he wanted to show her uncle were worthy of note. She could not deny him. "You and I shall take the stools and Uncle James will have the chair. I've some biscuits too if anyone would like some."

"What kind of biscuits?" Mr. Gibbs asked with a boyish smile.

"I've got vanilla and chocolate from the bakery next door," Ada said as she went to collect a tin. "They're both rather good."

She popped the lid on the tin, set it aside and offered Mr. Gibbs the biscuits. He selected a vanilla flavored one and Ada chose the same after letting Uncle James pick his. She placed the tin on a side table within easy reach before lowering herself to a stool. Her knee bumped Mr. Gibbs's and she muttered a hasty apology.

"So," said Uncle James before the situation could get more awkward, "how does a gentleman such as yourself pass his day when he's not visiting bookshops?"

Mr. Gibbs shrugged one shoulder and sipped his tea before saying, "I'd prefer to tell you how I ought to pass it rather than how I actually do – or have been, of late. Truth is I've been negligent in my duties for longer than I care to admit and must now face the consequences. My sisters, for instance, deserve to have debuts with all the pomp Society will expect on account of their stations. And then there are my properties, which all require servants and some sort of general upkeep. It's rather expensive and overwhelming."

"I'm sure you'll manage," Ada said. "I mean, you are a duke."

Mr. Gibbs produced an unhappy sort of laugh. "Yes, but such an elevated position has certain expectations attached to it. My sisters, for instance, cannot make their debuts without having different gowns for each event. And only the very best gowns, mind you. To say nothing of riding habits, shoes, bonnets, hats, gloves, reticules, shawls and…well, the list does go on."

"It sounds dreadful," Uncle James mused.

"It is," Mr. Gibbs said. He popped his vanilla biscuit into his mouth and chewed, then brushed a few stray crumbs from his mouth with the back of his hand. "Papa did a much better job of it than I have managed so far. He was a clever man who possessed an instinctive knack for investments and figuring out where to save and where not to. His death caught me completely off guard. I wasn't prepared. So rather than embrace my new duties, I ignored them, and here we are. I may be a duke, but only in name. As far as accomplishments go, I'm completely inept."

"I doubt that's true," Ada said, hoping to cheer him. Surely it couldn't be quite as bad as he let on.

"The important thing," Uncle James added, "is that you've acknowledged your mistake and that you are now prepared to do better."

"Which is incidentally part of my reason for stopping by today," Mr. Gibbs said. "The others being your exceptional company and these wonderful biscuits."

Ada smiled, catching his gaze just long enough to send her pulse racing. Ah, this man. If only he weren't so perfectly unattainable. This was the sort of man she might envision herself marrying.

Good lord. Now there's a line of thought that has to end this instant.

The shop bell chimed to let everyone know a new customer had arrived. Uncle James stood. "Please excuse me. I'll be back in a moment."

Ada almost protested the closing of the door when Uncle James left, but since she'd no desire for the customer to spot her with Mr. Gibbs, she chose to frown at it instead. Being alone with a man was the one thing all young ladies were told to avoid, yet here she was.

"I brought these," Mr. Gibbs said as though undaunted by their situation. "It would please me greatly if you'd take a look."

She tore her gaze from the door and saw that he held a pile of paper toward her. "What's this?"

He shoved it closer to her. "You should probably take it before I change my mind."

Amused and curious, she set her teacup aside and did as he asked. A bold script adorned the front and back of each page, of which there were possibly thirty in total. At the top of the first page was written, 'Chapter One'.

Intrigued, Ada proceeded to read, allowing herself to become engrossed in a story that featured a wealthy earl with an interest in horses. And, possibly, a lady of equal station, whom he seemed inclined to marry.

"Well?" Mr. Gibbs asked once she was finished reviewing what constituted three chapters.

"Um…" She sent him a hesitant look.

"That awful?" He'd visibly slumped on his stool with his forearms resting on his thighs while he stared at the floor with a frown.

She offered him the tin of biscuits and he happily took a chocolate one this time. "It's not awful. The descriptions are good, but I'm struggling to care about what happens next. The hero's life is charmed, as is the heroine's. They have no obstacles in their way, so why not have him propose to her on page one and be done with it?"

"Because then there'd be no story," Mr. Gibbs told her as though she were daft.

She grinned. "Right, but for a story to be compelling, there has to be conflict. In a romance novel, which is what I presume this to be, there must be something keeping the hero and heroine apart. For instance, the hero's family might have a long-standing dispute with the heroine's, like in *Romeo and Juliet*. Or maybe the heroine is already engaged to another man – perhaps to the hero's best friend."

"That would be nearly impossible to untangle."

"Yes, but finding a way to do so while leaving the reader guessing will produce the page-turner every author hopes to write." She handed the pages back to him. "I trust you wrote this?"

He nodded. "My friends and I desperately require a steady income, so when you mentioned a need for more books of this nature, I thought it might be a good opportunity."

Warmth filled the space surrounding Ada's heart. It was uncanny how much it pleased her to know that Mr. Gibbs hadn't merely chosen to heed her advice, but that he'd come to seek her opinion on the first few chapters he'd written.

"And it is," Ada said since she firmly believed this to be true.

"Maybe for someone with greater skill than what we possess." His brow was creased by serious lines. "To be honest, I knew it wasn't perfect, but I didn't imagine feeling as though we've wasted the last three days working on this."

Ada understood him. "I realize my critique might be dissuasive, but I'm hoping you don't give up trying because of what I've just said."

"I told my friends we could have the first draft completed within a month if we worked together, with an aim at publication a couple of months after that." He expelled a weary sigh. "Perhaps this time would be better spent trying to find other means of earning an income."

"Is your situation truly as dire as all that?" She was struggling to believe it.

He caught her gaze. "We've all squandered our fortunes and must resort to auctioning off some of our possessions in order to make ends meet. But there's a limit to how much we can get rid of before we make a mockery of ourselves. There are certain expectations linked to our titles that must be met. So we're trying to be discreet for the sake of keeping up appearances. Obviously, regular employment would be out of the question, but this was a viable option. It's just a lot harder than I'd imagined."

"Story telling is no simple feat." Ada worried her lower lip while deciding how best to proceed. Although it was probably very unwise for her to spend additional time in his company, she wanted to lend Mr. Gibbs her assistance. Would her heart survive it? Only time would tell. One thing was certain and that was that she'd begun to care about him. She couldn't therefore in good conscience turn her back on him when he needed her most. Decision made, she said, "I'm happy to help."

"You are?"

"Absolutely." She tapped her chin with her index finger while studying him. "Unfortunately, it will require starting over."

CHAPTER SEVEN

Anthony watched in fascination as Miss Quinn jotted down notes on a notepad she'd collected. Her opinion of his writing had been both insightful and tough to hear. He'd thought the story he and his friends had come up with so far was much better than it apparently was. Listening to Miss Quinn point out the flaws had swiftly changed his standing on this.

The story was off to a boring start. Which meant there was work to be done. Lots of it.

"As I mentioned," she said, "you need an obstacle between the hero and heroine. The more insurmountable this obstacle, the better. Readers should wonder how this man and woman will ever be able to bridge the divide between them and find the happily ever after they both deserve. So let's start there. Any ideas?"

Anthony blinked. He considered the pure intensity with which Miss Quinn approached this new task. Her determination to help him coupled with the warmth and comfort he always felt when in her presence were enticing. A pity she was no more than a shopkeeper's niece or he'd offer to court her in a heartbeat.

That wish, along with the purposeful beat it brought to his heart, was too poignant to be ignored. He gave a slow nod. "What if the earl were to fall for"—using shopkeeper would be too obvious—"a maid or an innkeeper's daughter."

"A class differences story?" Miss Quinn's eyes twinkled with undeniable pleasure. "I like that a lot. It could be similar to *Cinderella*. If we use the innkeeper idea, the heroine might receive assistance from an older woman who comes to stay for a while. A fairy godmother type who helps her transform. Or maybe the heroine learns that she's secretly the daughter of a baron, or a long-lost relation of the Prince Regent, or maybe…what? Why are you laughing?"

Anthony shook his head. "I'm simply enjoying myself, Miss Quinn. Please, do carry on."

She pursed her lips in the most adorable way, tempting him to lean in and kiss her.

He refrained and then her uncle returned, reminding Anthony of the late hour. He ought to leave.

"I think we're finally heading in the right direction," Miss Quinn informed him when he thanked her for the tea and stood. "You should keep working on this, but I would advise you to read Miss Austen's books too so you get a firm grasp of what readers expect."

"That is excellent advice, though it does have one problem." He tucked the papers he'd brought inside his jacket pocket along with the notes she'd made. "My editions have yet to arrive."

"Ah. Right."

"Anything I can help with?" Uncle James asked.

"Not unless you happen to have a spare copy of *Pride and Prejudice* lying about," Miss Quinn said.

Her uncle rocked back on his heels. "Can't say I do, but if it's an urgent matter, why not lend him yours?"

Miss Quinn pressed her lips together while seeming to consider. She glanced at Anthony, who did his best to keep his features schooled and to not give away how much he hoped she'd agree. The very idea of closing himself away for the evening with one of her books had the most profound effect. His muscles tightened and sparks of awareness ignited against his skin, no doubt on account of the intimacy related to the gesture.

"Very well," she said and promptly spun on her heel. Swiftly, she climbed the steep stairs near the back entrance and disappeared from Anthony's view.

"Care to share your reason for needing the book?" Mr. Quinn asked once he and Anthony were alone.

"It's supposed to be inspirational. I'm trying to write a novel, you see, and your niece suggested I research the sort of stories I'm aiming for."

"An excellent idea." Mr. Quinn sought Anthony's gaze and held it. "I'm glad you're here. Getting Ada out of the house has been a struggle. She refused to consider marriage when she was old enough to start looking for a potential match. Her sisters have wed but I think Ada feels she ought to stay here and help me. She has her own life to live though. Deuced hard convincing her of it, but then you came along and I did have some hope. Until we found out who you are and all that."

Despite Anthony's interest in Miss Quinn, he was slightly taken aback by her uncle's blatant suggestion pertaining to marriage. Unsure of how to respond, he chose to navigate around it by saying, "Again, I apologize for the deception."

"Oh no. I didn't mean it like that. As far as that goes, I quite understand. It simply would have been grand if you and she were able to... Well, never mind." He waved his hand and then Miss Quinn was scrambling back downstairs, forcing an end to the conversation.

Still, it had left Anthony reeling with a distinct sense of loss. He tried to shake it off but the truth was, he knew he wouldn't be rid of it until he knew he would see Miss Quinn again – that the promise of spending more time with her lingered upon the horizon.

Maybe he was being stupid, but the connection he felt with her could not be denied. So he took the book she handed him and said, "Thank you for your company and for all the advice you've offered. I promise to return this to you as soon as possible, and when I do, I hope to provide you with some much better pages for you to read."

A lovely pink hue tinged her cheeks. "I shall look forward to it, Mr. Gibbs."

He nodded, thanked her uncle for his hospitality too, and departed with a sense of contentment expanding his chest.

Mooning over Mr. Gibbs was a terrible mistake.

Ada told herself so repeatedly in the days that followed. She had to stop and yet there was no avoiding the thoughts she kept having. Not when his large body had dwarfed the interior of this very room where she now worked. He'd sat on that exact stool, placed his teacup right there, touched the tin of biscuits she'd eaten from ever since parting ways with him last.

She swept her brow with her hand and told herself to focus. He was a duke – possibly a poor one – but a duke nonetheless, and she was what exactly? A normal, everyday nobody without even the paltriest dowry to help her get settled.

If that was what she wished to do, which it wasn't.

Here with Uncle James she could have some degree of freedom.

Ha! The sort that involved hiding from the world and keeping her work a secret. What sort of freedom was that?

The sort that saved her from living under a husband's thumb as her sister, Dorothy, was forced to do. She had been an outspoken woman who'd lost her voice the moment she and her husband said, "I do."

Ada shook her head. She'd rather live in the back room of Between the Pages for the remainder of her days than suffer such a terrible fate. Although she imagined life with Mr. Gibbs might be different. He did seem like the sort of man who would listen to her opinions rather than always subject her to his own.

Ugh!

If only she could stop thinking about him.

She shook her head and finished the lettering on

the books she'd been completing. Uncle James would be dropping them off to a Mayfair address later today. It pleased Ada to see how well his shop was doing and made a mental note to thank Emily once again for constantly singing its praises in her column.

But whatever pleasure she felt was reduced to self-criticism later when Uncle James returned with the books he'd gone to drop off.

"There's a mistake with the binding," he told her, setting the books on the table.

Ada stared at the deep red shade of leather adorned with gold leaf. "What?"

"Mr. Wilkes has demanded we re-do both volumes at our own expense."

"I'm so sorry, Uncle James. I've no idea what happened. "

Not entirely true. Her head had been in the clouds since the day Mr. Gibbs walked into the shop. Or maybe she hadn't recovered from the blow to her head yet. Either way, meeting him - thinking of him - was bad for business. If she weren't careful, she'd ruin the shop's reputation. One mishap might be excusable with a loyal client, but if it happened again, word would undoubtedly start to spread. Customers would stop coming and Uncle James's income would suffer.

She could not allow that to happen after all he had done for her.

"You needn't look so torn up, Ada." He placed a hand on her shoulder. "Mistakes happen."

"I'll fix it," she whispered. "I promise."

"And I'm sure Mr. Wilkes will be thrilled with the result."

"Let's hope so." Ada stared at the lettering. The books were *The History of British India*, volumes one, two, and three, but she'd printed *Rob Roy* across the covers.

"Imbecile," she muttered as soon as Uncle James had gone back to the shop. Honestly, she could kick herself over the wasted time and money she'd caused.

Well, best get on with correcting her error. She grabbed a sharp knife and set to work, spending the rest of the day and much of the next one removing the leather binding she'd initially created and replacing it with a new one. This time, she took extra care to make sure the title on the cover matched the book itself before handing it over to her uncle for delivery.

"The duke is back," Uncle James informed her the following day when he came to find her. With no current work to complete, she'd decided to give the apartment a thorough cleaning and was in the middle of wiping the skirting. "He's asking to see you, so I thought you might take a break and come down?"

Ada pushed back onto her haunches and glanced at her uncle. "I'm not sure that's a good idea."

Uncle James scratched his head. "I thought you enjoyed his company."

There was no denying the dismay in his voice.

"And I do. Very much so." Too much, she'd concluded. She stood and dropped the cloth she'd been using into a pail filled with water and soap suds. "But look what his coming here has led to. As lovely as his visits have been, he's proven to be a distraction. I think he's the reason I messed up the Wilkes order."

"Ada…"

"It's probably best if you give Mr. Gibbs my regrets."

Uncle James stared at her. "Are you certain, Ada?"

"Quite." What use was there in spending more time with him anyway? It wasn't as if he'd suddenly choose to think, 'Ah yes, that woman who lives above a book shop would make me an excellent duchess. I must propose at once.'

She waited for Uncle James to leave before dropping back onto her knees with a huff. If she wrung out her cloth and continued cleaning with increased aggression, it was only because she was frustrated by all the dust that had gathered. Truly, it was a miracle they didn't continuously sneeze, she decided.

"He returned this," Uncle James said that afternoon when they met for tea in the back room as usual. He set her copy of *Pride and Prejudice* on her work table.

Ada stared at the two volumes comprising the novel. "What did he think of it?"

"I can't say." Uncle James snatched a chocolate biscuit from the tin she offered and took a bite. "He refused to tell me."

"What do you mean he refused?"

"He said you'd have to ask him yourself if you wanted to know."

"But maybe *you* wanted to know."

Uncle James glanced at the ceiling. "He's not daft, Ada."

"I never suggested he was," she muttered while sending her favorite novel a disgruntled frown. "What else did he say?"

"Just that he's got some new material for you to look at. I believe that's why he came – to ask your opinion and to hand the book back to you."

She bit into the biscuit she'd selected and chewed on it before saying, "He read it quickly. That's surely a positive sign."

Uncle James sighed. "Honestly, you'll have to ask him yourself if you truly want to know."

She pressed her lips together. "I don't think that's wise."

"Suit yourself, Ada."

"You're not going to try and change my mind?" Ada asked, eyeing him with suspicion.

"Would it work?"

"Probably not."

"Didn't think so." He ate the rest of his biscuit and washed it down with a large gulp of tea. "You've always been rather bull-headed. Even with the binding. Wouldn't let me talk you out of giving it a go. But I must confess I'm sorry to see you push Mr. Gibbs away. He's a good man and while he might not be in a position to think of you as a possible match, he could be a wonderful life-long friend."

Uncle James wasn't wrong, but unfortunately the risk he posed to her heart outweighed whatever benefit she might find in continuing their acquaintance. "I'm sorry, but I've made my decision."

"Well then, you ought to be pleased to know that the *Britannica* order was placed today."

"Emily stopped by?" She'd been looking forward to her visit. "Why didn't you say so?"

"She arrived while Mr. Gibbs was here. I could hardly show her up while turning a duke away, could I?"

"I suppose not," Ada muttered.

"The good news is that her order will give you a lot of binding to do. Twenty volumes worth, to be exact."

"I look forward to it," Ada lied. For the first time ever, book binding held no appeal. She wasn't excited about it. If anything, she had the most ridiculous urge to go back to bed and stay there for the foreseeable future. Her heart ached and she started to worry she might be coming down with a cold or, heaven help her, influenza.

But when a week went by with no worsening symptoms, she realized her new despondency might be caused by something else. Curiously, she felt slightly better whenever her uncle informed her that Mr. Gibbs had once again come to call upon her. He did so daily while she continued to make up excuses not to see him.

The Austen books he'd ordered arrived, so she took a break from the encyclopedia to work on those for a while. Once they were ready, she handed them over to Uncle James for delivery.

"He brought you these today," Uncle James informed her one evening when they met for supper. In his hand he held a massive bouquet of white roses.

Ada stared at the flowers. "What?"

"There's a note attached." He handed it to her before going to find a vase.

Befuddled and with her heart hopping about, Ada opened the card and read.

I saw these and thought of you. Anthony Gibbs.

It was ridiculous how happy a bouquet of flowers could make a woman, Ada decided, sniffing the fragrant perfume and admiring each perfect bloom. She felt slightly giddy and more excited than she probably ought.

Perhaps she should agree to see him when he stopped by next, to thank him at least.

No, it was too dangerous. He'd only muddle her head even worse. These flowers alone were enough to make her wonder if he might be thinking of her a little bit more than he probably ought. With the encyclopedia's delivery date on the horizon, she had to remain focused.

"I hope you'll tell him how grateful I am," Ada told Uncle James.

"You ought to do so yourself," he pointed out.

"Possibly, but I think it's best if I don't."

Her uncle responded with a snort and a shake of his head.

"Ada," he said the next morning, popping his head into the back room, "I need your help out here."

She'd been cutting the leather for the fifth volume in Emily's order but quickly put her supplies down and wiped her hands clean. When she entered the shop, she froze. Three bouquets of flowers stood on the counter, filling the space completely.

"What's this?" she asked.

"Here's the note," Uncle James informed her and handed over a cream-colored card. "We need to clear these out of here before customers start asking questions."

"Right. Of course." She grabbed one bouquet – a lovely display of pink peonies mixed with orchids. It smelled divine and made her head feel a little bit fuzzy.

Ada turned her attention to the card as soon as all the flowers had been brought into the back room.

It occurred to me that you might not be partial to roses, so I thought I'd send you these as well. Anthony Gibbs.

She stared at the words, re-reading them numerous times before setting the card aside. What on earth was he playing at? If she didn't know any better, she'd think he was trying to declare himself, but that couldn't be right. Surely. Then again, unmarried men did not send flowers to unmarried women unless they had intentions. Did they?

Afraid of getting her hopes up, Ada carried the flowers upstairs and placed them on various tables in the apartment.

"I really think you should see him, Ada," Uncle James told her the following day when additional bouquets arrived. "At this rate, there's more concern of creating gossip because of the flowers than because of any mistakes you might make with the binding."

He wasn't wrong, Ada decided. She crossed her arms and scowled at the collection of dahlia, lilies, gladioli, freesia, and additional roses. There were five bouquets this time. Five! She shook her head and wondered for the hundredth time what Mr. Gibbs might be aiming for.

Plucking a card from one of the bouquets she read his latest note.

Whatever I may have done to earn your disfavor, I apologize and beg your forgiveness. Anthony Gibbs.

Ada's heart shuddered. He thought she was upset with him for some reason. And why wouldn't he? She hadn't explained herself but had merely decided to stop associating with him from one day to the next. Of course he'd be confused.

Ada's heart raced as she realized the gravity of her mistake.

Lord, she was a bigger fool than she'd even thought possible. Self-absorbed came to mind too, which really wasn't a very flattering way to view oneself.

Expelling a weary breath, she turned to Uncle James. "I think I'd better speak with him."

"Thank you." Uncle James raised both hands toward the ceiling as if to convey that his prayers had been answered. Dropping them to his sides he told her gravely, "I know you have your apprehensions, but you mustn't worry. I'll double check all your work before we deliver it just to be sure no further mistakes arise. All right?"

Seeing no other choice, she agreed and prepared to do what should have been done several days before.

CHAPTER EIGHT

Anthony was perfectly aware of the fact that the large collections of flowers he'd sent to Between the Pages might have been slightly over the top. He probably ought to have saved the expense which now meant he'd have to cut back on other purchases for a whole week.

One bouquet, possibly two, or maybe three, would surely have been enough. But he'd been beside himself and had wanted to prove a point.

I like you a lot, was the general message he'd meant to convey.

Truth was, it was quite a bit more than that.

He mourned the loss of Miss Quinn's company, the conversations they'd shared, that spark of awareness he felt when they were together, and the delightful anticipation of their paths crossing once more.

Not to mention the wonderful help she'd provided. He'd conveyed her advice to Brody and Callum, and while they'd been just as unhappy as he to start over, they'd agreed it was necessary.

Pride and Prejudice had also been useful. Miss Quinn had been quite correct to make him read it. But she herself had suddenly put a halt to their newfound friendship. Without so much as an explanation.

When he'd asked her uncle if he could provide some insight, the man had, much to Anthony's aggravation, merely shrugged his shoulders and said he'd no idea why his niece chose not to see him. Only that she was busy.

Busy.

That was the lousiest excuse Anthony knew. However busy Miss Quinn might be, she surely had enough time to let him return her book. The task need not have taken more than five minutes at most.

But no. She'd shut the door and closed herself off, leaving him with very little recourse when it came to getting her attention.

He grinned as he re-read the note he'd received from her that afternoon. Apparently, he'd met with success.

My determination is clearly no match for yours. I look forward to seeing you at your convenience. Ada Quinn.

Perfect. He had her given name now as well.

The notion filled his chest with a warm sort of

bubbly sensation. It wasn't satisfaction, precisely, but something more that he couldn't quite find the word for.

Crossing to his desk, he set her note down and proceeded to write one of his own.

Miss Quinn, I am delighted to hear from you though I am still at a loss with regard to your reason for cutting me off. It is my sincerest hope that you will explain yourself to me when we meet again. If it suits you, we'll have a picnic this coming Saturday afternoon with my fellow authors in Green Park. I'll pick you up at three. In the meantime, I am including a re-write of what my friends and I have decided to name, A Seductive Scandal, *for your perusal.*

Respectfully,

Anthony Gibbs.

When no protestation to his proposal arrived in the following days, Anthony collected the picnic basket he'd ordered and set off Saturday afternoon with an extra bounce to his stride. It was curious how thrilled he was by the prospect of seeing Miss Quinn again, of chatting with her and spending a full afternoon in her company.

It wasn't a romantic outing, he reminded himself. He'd been careful to make sure Brody and Callum would be there too. So Miss Quinn wouldn't worry about him being too pushy after the flowers. But the way he felt told a different story from what he'd chosen to put on display.

Miss Quinn was special, the connection he'd experienced with her each time they'd met as unique as each puffy cloud in the sky. Truth was, he wanted more than friendship with her, but how was he to accomplish such a feat? Would she even welcome such a change to their relationship?

For now, he decided to keep things simple. She'd agreed to meet and this was a start. Wherever things went from there, he'd deal with it in due course.

"She's waiting for you in the back," Mr. Quinn informed Anthony when he arrived. The older man smiled, sent the door to the back room a hasty glance, and whispered, "Thank you for not giving up."

"I wouldn't dream of it," Anthony said as he hefted the large picnic basket onto the counter and blew out a breath. Then choosing to speak from the heart, he quickly added, "Some things are worth pursuing forever."

"I'm glad you think so," Mr. Quinn said. He crossed to the door and opened it, allowing Anthony to catch a glimpse of Miss Quinn. She was standing with her back toward him, her hands on her hips, and her attention seemingly riveted by a large book bound in black leather. "Mr. Gibbs has arrived, Ada."

Miss Quinn spun to face them, the look on her face suggesting she'd not heard them enter. Her lips parted, increasing her flustered appearance. She seemed to shake it off and begin searching the room.

"Oh. Good. I'll, um…just grab my bonnet. And my reticule. Maybe a shawl as well?"

Anthony dipped his head, chin to chest, and pressed his lips together to keep from laughing. Unfortunately, he feared his shoulders might be shaking too much to hide his mirth. She truly was the most adorable creature he'd ever encountered.

"Ready?" he asked once she'd managed to wrap herself in a fringed length of cotton and had hidden most of her lovely blonde hair beneath a straw bonnet with a brim so large he could no longer see her eyes.

"Quite so."

He sent her a smile and went to collect the picnic basket. Given the weight of the blasted thing, it probably would have been wise to send it ahead by carriage. Anthony tightened his grip on the handle and did his best to simultaneously open the shop door, holding it wide so Miss Quinn could exit.

They set off arm in arm, with Anthony wondering how best to broach the subject that pressed most firmly upon his mind. Eventually, he gave up trying to find a delicate way to ease into it, choosing instead to be direct.

"Will you please put me out of my misery and tell me why you began avoiding me?" He adjusted his hold on the basket. It was proving a cumbersome hindrance to a smooth pace.

She was quiet a moment before confessing, "I worried you might be bad for business."

He choked. "I beg your pardon?"

"It was wrong to push you away without explanation," she added. "Truth is, I've enjoyed your company tremendously, which is something rather unique for me since I do not make friends easily."

"Go on," he encouraged when she fell silent for a long while. They crossed the street and turned a corner, bringing the park entrance into view. The iron gate stood open, inviting Londoners in.

"Uncle James began having some health problems a few years ago," Miss Quinn began. "His joints stiffen and hurt, so I've been helping him more than what would be deemed proper."

"You're referring to the book binding?"

She stumbled a little but he kept her upright. Her gaze rose to his, allowing him to see her wide-eyed expression. "How long have you known?"

He drew her closer to his side. "Since I placed the order for Miss Austen's books."

"Please don't tell anyone. It's bad enough that I'm living above the bookshop. If it becomes known that I'm binding books, it could bring scandal upon the shop's name."

"I think that's ridiculous when you're obviously very skilled." He eyed her. "Especially since I've heard of other women being engaged in such trade."

"Married women, Mr. Gibbs. Or widowed ones."

She hardened her expression. "It's not considered appropriate for unmarried women to engage in such things."

"Of course not," Anthony told her dryly. "They might find forbidden knowledge between the pages of all these books and learn more than their brains can safely process. Or worse, have their souls corrupted."

"You jest, but it is indeed a valid concern." She directed her gaze toward the park entrance as they approached it, effectively hiding her eyes and most of her face from his view. "The book shop is Uncle James's bread and butter. I'll not put it at risk."

"And you shouldn't, but I'm still not sure how your acquaintance with me could possibly do so."

She sighed. "I hope you won't put too much stock in what I'm about to reveal, but the fact is I messed up an order last week. It was horribly embarrassing. I cannot even imagine how awful it must have been for Uncle James to take the blame. Fortunately the customer was a loyal one who was willing to ignore the mishap as long as we fixed the error at our own cost."

"I see." Strike that. Anthony wasn't sure he saw the logic in any of this at all. "What was the mistake?"

"I labeled *The History of British India* by James Mills, *Rob Roy* instead."

"Huh…" Realization struck and he drew her to a

halt beneath the park gate, maneuvering them to one side so they didn't block the path. "You were distracted."

"I was."

"By me."

The truth and what it implied hovered between them like a fat albatross trying to find enough space on which to land. Despite her large bonnet, he saw her scrunch the tip of her nose. Adorable. It was impossible for him to keep from smiling. How could he when she'd just confessed he'd been on her mind a lot more than what he would have been if she thought of him as only a friend?

His smile broadened. "If it helps, I've thought of you too. At great length. Day and night."

She shook her head just enough to convey that this did not help her in the least. "What am I supposed to do with that information?"

He stared at her. "I'm not entirely sure."

She huffed a breath. "Perhaps we ought to discuss your story instead? I believe it might prove more productive than our current conversation."

"All right." They entered the park and followed a path that would take them to the out of the way spot where his friends had agreed to meet them. The air was pleasant, not too warm nor too cold, though one might think it overly chilly judging from Miss Quinn's attire.

Anthony frowned at her while doing his best to

carry the unwieldy basket the last of the distance. At some point he'd have to encourage her to unravel that shawl.

"Good day, Your Grace," someone said, drawing his attention to Baron Deerford who was strolling in the opposite direction with his wife.

Anthony greeted the couple while noting their curious gazes – most notably directed at Ada – and quickly steered her past them.

"Your story is much improved from the previous version I read," she told him, seemingly oblivious to the brief bit of attention they'd garnered. "I enjoyed the opening chapters a great deal and look forward to learning what happens next."

Her comment made it easy for him to ignore the curious glances the rest of the parkgoers sent their way. His chest expanded, allowing warmth to pour in and fill him with pleasure. "Truly?"

"Yes. The hero and heroine are both compelling and there's now the question of how they'll manage to breach the divide between them."

Anthony's lips quirked. "I'll admit I'm not sure how we'll do it just yet. Any advice you'd like to give would be most welcome."

"Well, he is an earl with certain expectations attached to his status. Falling for an innkeeper's daughter is inconvenient. I suppose he'll have to make a difficult choice at some point toward the end. There's his reputation on one hand and the woman he loves on the other."

Anthony's heart gave a quick little kick in response to that word. He slowed his pace, forcing her to slow hers as well. Love. The most complicated emotion of all.

"How will he know?" He voiced the question without even thinking.

She raised her chin just enough to let him glimpse the curious look in her lovely blue eyes. "That he loves her?"

His chest tightened. "Precisely."

"I suppose you'll want to have him missing her when they're apart, wondering about her well-being, possibly even fretting over her if she falls ill, or wanting to move both heaven and earth to make her happy. As Darcy does by helping Elizabeth's sister, Lydia, out of her bind with Wickham. Doing so went against his pride, but he did it for her, to save her family's reputation. It was a grand gesture of love made all the more so because he did not seek to be recognized for it."

"You truly love that book, don't you?" When she grinned and turned her face upward, he told her, "There's a glow about you whenever you speak of it. I find it extremely compelling."

"If luck will have it, many readers will speak of your book in the same way one day. I've faith in you, Mr. Gibbs, and in your friends."

Her enthusiasm was infectious. It made him feel as he'd done the first time he'd caught a young lady's notice. Grinning, he steered Miss Quinn toward the spot where Brody and Callum sat. Relieved to set the picnic basket down, he proceeded to make the introductions.

"We've heard a great deal about you, Miss Quinn," Brody said. The hint of amusement in his eyes caused heat to wash the back of Anthony's neck. "Apparently you're a wealth of information with regard to romantic novels."

"I was personally shocked when Anthony suggested we write one," Callum said, "but his reasoning – for which I gather he has you to thank – made sense. We've become quite invested, actually. Now that we've begun, the ideas keep coming."

"I'm glad to hear it," Miss Quinn said, the hesitance in her voice reminding Anthony that she was not used to meeting strangers.

Seemingly unsure about what to say, she took a seat on one of the two blankets Callum and Brody had brought. Anthony lowered himself beside her while his friends sat opposite. A few nearby bushes and trees shielded them slightly from the footpath, adding a bit more privacy than if they'd chosen the more open space near the park entrance.

"We're very eager to hear you opinion," Brody told Ada.

She cleared her throat and sent Anthony a quick

glance. When he gave an encouraging nod, she said, "As I was telling Mr. Gibbs on the way ov—"

"Mr. Gibbs?" Brody gaped at her, then at Anthony, before quickly collecting himself. "Sorry. Um… You were saying?"

"He was Mr. Gibbs when we met," Miss Quinn explained, her voice faltering slightly as though with uncertainty. "Feels strange referring to him by a different name now."

"Agreed," Anthony said in an effort to make her feel more at ease.

"I'm intrigued," Callum said with a smirk. "Do go on."

"I'll fill you in later," Anthony told him when he saw the high color in Ada's cheeks. He sent his friend a look of warning before gently addressing her. "Please continue."

"Oh… Um…" She fidgeted with her skirt. "As I mentioned to him on our way over, I'm quite impressed by your latest attempt at a novel. It's compelling and I want to know more. What happens next, for instance?"

Anthony pulled the picnic basket into the middle of the circle they'd formed and opened it. "I'm not sure we know, which is part of the problem. Right now, our biggest issue is figuring out how the hero and heroine end up together."

He went over the comments Miss Quinn had made on that score while Brody and Callum helped set up the tea he'd brought. "Basically, the hero has to choose the heroine no matter the cost to his reputation."

"Which makes me wonder if his reputation presents a big enough obstacle for them," Miss Quinn mused.

"What?" Anthony, Brody, and Callum all asked in unison.

"If the hero has enough self-esteem and a decent circle of friends willing to lend their support, what difference does it make to him what everyone else thinks?" Miss Quinn accepted the teacup Anthony handed to her with a softly spoken, "Thank you."

"Society's opinion is everything," Brody explained and promptly knit his brow. "I realize that sounds rather awful, but what other peers think, their good opinion or lack thereof, can determine one's future."

"Fall out of grace," Callum said, "and there's no telling what might occur. Doors could close, denying the connections upon which we all depend so heavily."

"And it's not just a question of how, um... marrying down will affect the earl," Anthony pointed out without being able to meet Miss Quinn's gaze, "but the consequence it may have upon those nearest and dearest to him."

"Family," Miss Quinn said with a thoughtful nod. "One does what one can to protect them and keep them out of harm's way. Perhaps this is an angle worth exploring in greater detail. Have you decided whether or not the earl has any siblings?"

"We considered a brother who's chosen a military career," Brody said.

"Why not include a younger sister – a lady with every conceivable chance of making an excellent match," Miss Quinn said while filling her cup with the tea Anthony offered. Her posture relaxed as she spoke. "Provided her brother doesn't create a scandal with his pursuit of an innkeeper's daughter."

It was impossible for Anthony to ignore the similarity she'd just created between the real situation he found himself in with her, and the fictional plot point she'd just provided. He wondered if she was aware of it. Probably not, he decided while studying the undeniable gleam of enthusiasm sparkling in her blue eyes.

"Sounds like a quagmire to me," Callum said as he reached for one of the sandwiches Anthony's cook had prepared.

Brody took one too. "How will we ever muddle our way through it?"

"I'm sure you'll figure it out," Miss Quinn said as she too took a sandwich. She smiled at Anthony, a brilliant smile that instilled in him a need to slay every dragon she might encounter. "Remember, you can take a few days to do so. The reader won't know you struggled. They'll just be impressed that you managed to pull it off."

All three men groaned, which apparently caused her to chuckle. It pleased him to watch her shed the discomfort she'd shown when they'd first arrived here.

"You're enjoying this, aren't you?" Anthony asked, attempting to keep his voice light and teasing.

She grinned. "Guilty, I confess."

Sobering, she added, "I believe your greatest challenge will be writing three different parts of the same book simultaneously. The characters and their goals must remain constant."

"Which is why we've each got a copy of the plot outline," Brody said. "We've also agreed to meet once a day in order to review our progress."

Ada gave a thoughtful nod. "It's probably also wise of you to take notes of any new details being added so all of you are made aware of them."

"That's not a bad idea though it might slow things down." Callum sent her a wary look. "Your advice is good, Miss Quinn. So good I'm almost afraid to ask if you have any other ideas for how we might improve."

Miss Quinn pursed her lips as though in consideration. "With only three chapters completed, it's a little hard to say, but one important aspect will be your ability to bring love onto the page."

"How do you mean?" Brody asked.

"I believe the effect you want," Miss Quinn said, her words measured, "is for the reader to end the book with a sigh of pleasure. You want them to feel a happy sort of assurance that the characters fought their way through a tough situation and won."

Anthony leaned back so his hands and arms supported his upper body. "And how do you propose we accomplish that?"

Miss Quinn picked a blade of grass and twiddled it loosely between her fingers. "I suppose it can be done by showing how well the hero and heroine support each other. Even if their opinions differ, they should come together as a team. Compromise is key, I would think. And then of course there are the smaller gestures that come into play. If you drop a few hints here and there about something the heroine wants to experience, for example, and then have the hero help her do it, this would show that he's been paying attention to her, that he cares about her, and that her happiness matters to him. The same is true for her of course. If he visits the inn, for example, and mentions how sorry he is to learn that they no longer make the dessert he'd been hoping to try, she could ask him to wait while she goes and makes it."

"Hmm…" A pensive look had come over Brody's face. "I believe I'm starting to understand what you mean. Basically, we need to show the reader that these two are willing to do more for each other than what they might do for their friends or family."

"I'm sure they'd do a great deal for their family too," Miss Quinn said, "because they love them. The hero and heroine need to be included in that circle of love. The fiercer that love is, the greater the lengths they'll be willing to go to in order to stand by each other, the more powerful the experience will be for the reader."

"Your ability to clarify this is rather remarkable," Callum said with the same sense of awe Anthony had begun feeling toward her at some point since their first meeting. "It sounds like you speak from experience, so I hope you won't take offense to my asking if you've ever known such a love."

Anthony sucked in a breath and held it while doing his best to keep his expression neutral. It hadn't occurred to him until now that this might explain why Miss Quinn was so well versed in romance.

Her uncle had said she'd no interest in marriage, but maybe her stance on this had changed. Perhaps she had a secret beau. It was possible, given her age. And what if she did? Would it make any difference to Anthony?

Yes, was the resounding answer knocking about in his head.

She took a deep breath and chuckled lightly. "I'm afraid I've not been so lucky."

The relief washing through him was so intense he almost sagged beneath the weight of it. Thank God. Her heart remained unattached.

"I'm surprised," Brody said. "In light of your beauty and charm, I'd imagine you having a number of suitors."

Anthony scowled at him. The scoundrel would do well to flirt with anyone other than Miss Ada Quinn.

A pink hue darkened her cheeks. "I'm afraid not. Truth is they'd have a hard time meeting me in the first place, seeing as I rarely go anywhere. I'm not a social person and—"

"Westcliffe," a shrill voice called, much to Anthony's chagrin.

He turned to see Viscount Ebberly's dreaded daughter, Miss Amanda Starling, striding toward them with one of her friends. Dressed in a gown far too lavish for walking, the slim, petite blonde looked like a doll with her pale porcelain features framed by carefully arranged curls.

Suppressing a groan, Anthony excused himself to Miss Quinn and stood. As did Brody and Callum.

"Miss Starling," Anthony said, his mouth stretched into a tight smile. "What a surprise."

"Indeed it is," she purred as she came to stand before Anthony. "But not a sorry one, I must say. It's always a great pleasure to see you. You know my friend, Lady Edwina, of course."

Anthony gave both ladies a curt bow. "A pleasure."

Brody and Callum followed suit while Miss Quinn got up, so she too was now standing. Anthony gestured toward her. "Allow me to present my very good friend, Miss Quinn."

"Ah." Miss Starling raised her dainty nose and peered at Miss Quinn as though she were a flawed piece of art. "Delighted, I'm sure."

Anthony gnashed his teeth and prayed the woman would wish them all a good day and move on. Instead, she turned a dazzling smile on him. "I've written your sisters today as promised and have asked them to join me for tea on Saturday. In exchange, I trust you'll keep your end of the bargain?"

Anthony blinked at the reminder. Damn the bloody deal. He'd completely forgotten about it. So much had happened since, but he supposed he was grateful to her for paying his sisters attention. However much he dreaded Miss Starling setting her sights on him, he had to acknowledge the benefit of her acquaintance.

"I am a man of my word," Anthony told her, forcing the words out while doing his best not to look like he'd just bitten into a lemon.

"Then I shall look forward to seeing you again soon." She sent Miss Quinn a quick smile before leaning in to whisper, just loud enough for all to hear, "Papa has the marriage contract drawn up. All you need do is sign."

Anthony stood, rooted to the ground, unable to utter a word as she and her friend swept away.

"Marriage contract?" Brody asked, jolting Anthony out of his frozen state. "You can't be serious."

"I…um…" Anthony raked his fingers through his hair.

"You'll have to forgive me," Miss Quinn said, her voice a touch uneven. "It's getting late and I ought to return to the shop."

"But we've not had the cake yet," Anthony said. Turning toward her he noted the anxious look in her eyes right before she dipped her head to hide the emotion. "Please stay a while longer."

"I can't," she said. "I'm sorry. It's been a pleasure meeting you both, Your…um…Graces?"

Brody grinned. "The pleasure was entirely ours, I assure you, Miss Quinn."

"If you give me a moment to gather everything," Anthony said, already lowering into a crouch and reaching for Miss Quinn's half empty teacup, "I'll escort you."

"There's really no need," she said, prompting him to glance up and to see the tight smile she wore. "I am perfectly able to find my way back. And as you have just said, there's still cake. I see no reason for my early departure to deny you and your friends."

"But—"

"Thank you for a wonderful afternoon, Mr. Gibbs. It has been most enlightening."

Anthony wanted to say something more. He wanted to leap to his feet and reach out and stop her. Clearly the interaction with Miss Starling and what it suggested had put her off. She was retreating from him and while he longed to explain his relationship with Miss Starling, he worried he might be leaping to the wrong conclusion.

For what if Miss Quinn's hasty departure had nothing to do with Miss Starling and everything to do with her obligation toward her uncle? She had made it clear that she could not stay out too long. So if he began explaining himself and what his relationship with Miss Starling entailed, she might believe him to be too forward.

By chasing after Miss Quinn and assuring her Miss Starling meant nothing to him, he would practically be declaring himself. And for what? In what sort of world could a duke find his happily ever after with a shopkeeper's niece who lacked connections?

"We're still waiting for an explanation," Brody said, disrupting Anthony's thoughts. "You cannot possibly mean to tell us that you're engaged to Miss Starling."

"I'm not," Anthony said. "It's complicated with her."

"No more so than it is with Miss Quinn, I'll

wager," Callum murmured. "She's lovely, by the way, and the two of you seem to get along famously."

His friend was spot on, but the situation was more than what he described. With Miss Quinn, Anthony felt relaxed and comfortable. Being with her was like being with someone he'd not even known he'd been missing. It was magical and it scared the living hell out of him.

CHAPTER NINE

There was no point in dissecting the conversation between Mr. Gibbs and Miss Starling, Ada decided. The situation was clear. They were engaged. To be married. All that remained was for him to sign the blasted contract. Which he would do. Because why on earth wouldn't he?

Miss Starling would make him a marvelous match. She was pretty, perfectly poised, and elegant in a way Ada could never hope to be. Most important of all, she was a somebody. Ada wasn't entirely sure what sort of somebody the lady was, but pedigree had wafted off her like a heavy perfume. It had been impossible to ignore, considering her fine gown, exquisite bonnet, diamond encrusted brooch, expensive parasol, and perfectly styled hair.

Ugh!

Ada dropped her head onto the work table and muttered a very unladylike curse.

Of course the one man she happened to meet and like and possibly—or rather definitely—dream about one day marrying would be firmly attached to another. It was just the sort of disastrous outcome she'd have expected if she were the heroine of her own novel. Except in that novel she'd somehow end up gloriously happy in the end. Reality, however, promised a far more dismal outcome.

She straightened and returned her attention to the distraction the encyclopedia offered. Each of the twenty volumes had now been beautifully bound. She was currently working on the spines, which she'd decided to complete before adding the title and volume number to the front cover.

Emily would be pleased. Ada was certain of it. The books comprised some of her best work to date and would be a handsome addition to Lord Rosemont's library.

She filled the next tray with letters and numbers, clamped the book into place, and pressed the heated stamp onto volume three's spine.

"This just arrived for you," Uncle James said, entering her work space before she managed to add the gold leaf. He held a white envelope toward her.

Ada stared at it for a brief second before setting her tools aside and accepting the missive. The lettering on the front was unfamiliar to her. It didn't look like Mr. Gibbs's and yet the stationary was quality. She glanced at her uncle. "Any idea who it's from?"

"None. It was hand delivered by courier, but I'll wager you might find out if you open it and read the contents."

She grabbed a sharp knife and broke the glossy red seal, then retrieved the thick card that had been tucked inside the envelope. Puzzled, she turned it over, unable to fathom what it was or that it had been sent to her.

"It's an invitation," she muttered. "To the Marquess of Axelby's ball, two weeks from today."

"Really?" Uncle James took the card from her and read it himself.

She shook her head. "It must be some sort of mistake."

"A curious one, considering both of our names are on it."

Baffled, Ada peered at the card Uncle James was holding. "It doesn't make any sense."

"Things don't always have to." Uncle James handed the invitation back to her. "But in this instance I'd hazard a guess that your Mr. Gibbs might be involved."

"First of all, he's not *my* Mr. Gibbs." If anything, he was Miss Starling's. "And second of all, I cannot believe he'd do so without informing us first."

"I'm no expert in such things, Ada, but I don't

believe it's common practice to warn people about invitations they might be receiving."

"Perhaps not." She set the invitation aside. "We obviously can't go."

Uncle James leaned back on his heels, arms crossed. "I don't see why not if we've been invited."

Ada gaped at him. "Neither one of us has the right clothes for such an event nor the polish required to mingle with aristocracy. We'd only embarrass ourselves, which is why I'm unhappy with this invitation. If Mr. Gibbs did procure it, he did so without any thought of the impact our showing up might have upon us. Clients of ours will most likely be there. Can you imagine how they will react if we show up?"

"To be honest, I hadn't really considered it. I'll agree that you may have a point. But, I'm also inclined to think the best of people instead of the worst. It's possible we might enjoy ourselves, and you might even gain additional admirers."

The hope in his eyes was crushing. "None that will want to court me once they realize I've got no fortune to speak of."

"You've got more of a fortune than you realize," Uncle James said with a sad sort of smile. "A pity you belittle yourself as much as you do."

She sighed. "You know what I mean, Uncle James. None of the people we'll find at the Axelby ball will care about my winning personality or how kind I might be. They'll only want to know who my father was and how much I might have inherited from him."

"And?" Uncle James gave her a pointed look that forced her to address the facts of her birthright.

"The answer to that is an idealistic adventurer and nothing." Papa had not possessed a title. Worse, he'd spent most of his money financing his travels. Fortunately for Ada's sisters, they'd been of marital age at the time, so he'd made plans for them. As such, they had both had decent dowries. Too bad Papa had believed there was plenty of time to make arrangements for Ada.

"He wasn't a complete nobody," Uncle James tried. "Your father was a gentleman. And I realize this may surprise you, but I am too."

"In name only."

"Which is all that really matters."

If only that were true. Ada, however, didn't believe it for one second. Mr. Gibbs was a duke. More than that, he needed money to finance his lifestyle and offer his sisters the futures they deserved. He could not give his attentions to a woman without means. Certainly not when Miss Starling obviously offered the sort of convenience he required.

"I'm of the opinion that you ought to think about this carefully," Uncle James advised. He placed his index finger upon the invitation and slid it toward her. "Don't make a hasty decision you might regret."

"Very well," she agreed, even though she already knew what she had to do. Sending her regrets was the only logical option – a decision she chose to share with her friends when they met for their next book club meeting.

"This is so unbelievably romantic," Harriet said with a sigh. She followed the comment by slapping Ada on the arm. "Why didn't you tell us you'd gained a duke's notice?"

"Because nothing can come of it." Ada glared at the cup of tea she'd been served. "I am who I am and he is who he is. We're an impossible match."

"The best fairytales feature impossible matches," Harriet insisted. "Obviously he's interested or he wouldn't have made sure you got invited. It's the perfect opportunity for him to ask you to dance."

"Which would result in disaster considering I've not had a dance lesson since I was little. Plus, I'm not a hundred percent sure the invitation was issued because of him. I've not seen him since the picnic I spoke of." She'd chosen not to mention the flower deliveries, just in case Harriet swooned and required smelling salts for her revival. One would think *she* were the one who'd gained a duke's notice.

"Can you think of anyone else who might be behind it?" Emily asked. "Just to be clear, I had nothing to do with this, Ada, though I do wish I had. But I'm not well enough acquainted with the marquess to make such a request. However, I do believe Westcliffe might be. For one thing, he has the command that comes with his title. For another, I've also seen the pair together on numerous occasions, so it's not a stretch to suppose he called in a favor."

"Not that it matters." Ada picked up her teacup and took a long sip while wishing it might have been spiked with something a little stronger than tea. "My showing up would be laughable. I wouldn't fit in."

"What does your uncle say?" Harriet asked. "His name was on the invitation as well."

Ada shrugged. "I believe he's all for it, but I'm not sure he realizes just how foolish we'll look."

Emily tilted her head and studied Ada a moment before saying, "He is gentry though, is he not?"

"Technically speaking, but he's been out of Society for as long as I can remember. After all, he did decide to do the unthinkable by using his inheritance to go into trade."

"Quite right," Emily murmured. "Unfortunately there are a great many members of the upper class who would frown upon such a thing."

"Which is why we cannot go." Ada slumped in her seat. "Uncle James is such a good man. His business is respectable. But I worry people will think he and I are stepping out of line – venturing into a world we do not belong in."

"And you're worried you'll be mocked for it," Harriet said, voicing the biggest concern Ada had been wrestling with since she'd received the invitation. She gave her friends a helpless look and nodded.

"I suppose your concern is legitimate," Emily said, but a thoughtful look in her eyes informed Ada that she was trying to plot a way through this tangle. "However, I shall be in attendance too, and I'm sure Papa will lend his support if I ask it of him. Between us, we'll protect you."

"That's awfully kind of you, Emily, but—"

"Westcliffe will too, I believe," said Harriet, her eyes glazed over by dreamy wonder.

"Not to mention Axelby," Emily added. "As host, it will be his duty to make sure you're both comfortable and that you're kept apart from anyone who might pose a threat."

"I don't know," Ada said. "It feels rather risky."

Harriet snatched a biscuit from a nearby plate. "Most things worth having involve risk in some form or other."

"Any number of things could go wrong," Ada told them both despite feeling as though her argument was starting to lose steam.

"The same can be said of crossing the street," Emily pointed out. "And if the next argument you plan on making relates to your clothes, you needn't worry. I'll have my maid hem one of my gowns by an inch and send it over."

"Emily, I couldn't possibly accept."

"As for your uncle," Emily said as though Ada

hadn't spoken, "I'm sure we can figure out something. My brother might be of a similar size. I'll have a word with him later when I get home."

Ada stared at her friend – a woman she'd known for less than a year. "I've no idea what to say. Thank you, Emily. Thank you ever so much."

"Does that mean you're going?" Harriet asked, reaching for another biscuit.

Ada produced a throaty laugh that caught her somewhat by surprise. "I suppose it does."

She smiled at her friends, hiding all her misgivings. Not just from them, but also from herself.

CHAPTER TEN

As much as he liked to pretend otherwise, Anthony's nerves were in chaos. Contrary to his usual habit of showing up fashionably late, he'd arrived at Axelby's home at eight o'clock sharp and had therefore been one of the first guests to enter the ballroom. It had been a great relief when Brody and Callum arrived, offering him an escape from the stilted conversation he'd been having with one of the older matrons.

Now, strategically positioned near the front of the room, he kept his gaze on the entrance while hoping Miss Quinn would show up. Naturally, Axelby had been surprised when he'd made the request to invite her and her uncle. He'd hesitated a tad too long for Anthony's liking, but in the end, he'd relented. They were longtime friends after all, and

Axelby did owe him a favor or two for covering for him when they'd been at Eton.

The orchestra started playing the first few notes of a reel. Additional couples arrived, filling the ball-room with lively chatter. Despite the anxiousness tensing his muscles, he felt more at ease than he'd done this past year. The horse he'd listed for sale two weeks prior had brought him twenty pounds. He'd sold two more since then, along with several items he'd found in the attic.

A painting by Rubens, tucked away at the bottom of a large trunk, had earned a staggering total of nearly two hundred pounds. Though he'd still need additional funds for his sisters' debuts, it was enough to pay his outstanding bills and cover all immediate expenses.

The discovery had prompted him to carefully assess the rest of the artwork he owned. As a man with little interest in art beyond what he found pleasing to the eye, he'd never really considered the worth of his own collection.

As with most of the things that filled his house and his country estate, they'd been handed down to him from previous generations. He'd grown up with them simply being there, and as a result, he'd not really spared them much thought. Until now.

"What do you think?" Brody asked.

Anthony stared at him. And at Callum. He'd no idea what they'd been talking about. "Forgive me, but I fear I got distracted for a moment and missed the subject of the conversation."

Callum grinned. "If I were mooning after a lady, I'd be distracted too."

"I'm not mooning over anyone," Anthony grumbled.

"There's no shame in it," Callum said. "We both think Miss Quinn is delightful."

Unfortunately, the next lady to arrive was not Miss Quinn but rather Miss Starling. Dressed in a pale blue gown and with her hair predictably styled to perfection, she entered the ballroom with her two younger sisters. Pausing briefly, she swept the room with her eagle-eyed gaze and quickly spotted her quarry – namely him.

Brilliant.

Anthony sighed. As payment for the tea she'd invited his sisters to attend, he'd enjoyed an unpleasant visit to The National Gallery with her earlier in the week. To make certain it wouldn't look as though they were courting, he had insisted on meeting her there and had chosen to bring his sisters along for the outing.

Unsurprisingly, Miss Starling had not looked the least bit pleased.

"If you step out onto the terrace, we'll stall her," Brody said, realizing Anthony's dilemma. "You can escape to the garden for a while. Just long enough for her dance card to fill."

Knowing Miss Starling, such a thing would be unlikely. She'd make sure to leave one spot vacant until he returned. The predatory gleam in her eyes as she started toward him was chilling. He was tempted to follow Brody's advice, if only to avoid speaking with her at great length. But what if Miss Quinn arrived during his absence?

"Your Graces," Miss Starling said, arriving before them too quickly. "What a delight it is to find the three of you already in attendance."

Anthony forced a smile while Callum and Brody both gave a short bow.

"You're looking particularly lovely this evening, Miss Starling," Callum told her smoothly.

"Why thank you." She smiled at them each in turn before letting her gaze meet Anthony's. "May I offer you my dance card, Your Grace?"

A prickly sort of discomfort erupted on Anthony's skin as she held the dreaded card toward him. Placed in a horrid position where turning her down would not only breach his agreement but also appear unspeakably rude, Anthony took the card with great reluctance and considered the choices. He knit his brow and clenched his jaw as he grabbed the pencil that had been attached with a creamy silk ribbon. Thankfully, she'd come to him first, which left all options open.

He placed his name next to a quadrille, which would hopefully lead to the least amount of contact between them. Good God, what had he been thinking when he'd asked Viscount Ebberly if she might be amenable to a possible match?

That particular conversation had clearly taken on a life of its own if a marriage contract had since been prepared. And contrary to his request, the viscount had clearly let details of Anthony's visit slip if Miss Starling now saw herself on the way to the altar with him.

It was awful and monstrously stupid on Ebberly's part to entertain such a notion without being certain it was something Anthony actually wished to go through with.

He handed the card back to Miss Starling and watched as the edge of her mouth dipped.

"Oh," she muttered. "I thought you'd select the waltz."

"On the contrary, I much prefer the quadrille." Even though he wanted to run toward the nearest exit, he kept himself perfectly still while offering her the blankest stare he could muster. "But if you'd rather not dance it with me then—"

"No, no," she quipped, her tone a touch too bright. "The quadrille will be lovely, I'm sure. I look forward to partnering with you, Your Grace."

Anthony was about to tell her something of a similar nature when a movement near the entrance caught his attention. His gaze shifted and then he saw her, the most dazzling woman he'd ever laid eyes on.

For a second, it was difficult for him to comprehend that it was actually she. It took his brain a moment to realize what his eyes had already acknowledged.

He sucked in a breath as his heart leapt with joy.

She'd come. Miss Quinn was here. And she looked incredible.

Dressed in a cream-colored gown sewn from layers of lace and adorned with beadwork, she sparkled like a newly polished diamond in the candlelight spilling from wall sconces and chandeliers. Blindingly beautiful came to mind, Anthony decided as he started forward, his attention fixed solely upon the lady who'd captured his every attention.

"Westcliffe," Miss Starling squeaked as he passed her. "Where are you going? You can't just—"

Hopeful that his friends would have the good sense to distract her, he ignored her completely while cutting a path directly toward Miss Quinn. Much to his relief, he reached her before any other young men had a chance to pull themselves together and approach the new arrival. Her uncle stood by her side, his expression curiously nostalgic as he glanced toward the dance floor.

Odd that, Anthony thought for the briefest moment, that a man who worked in a bookshop would enter a ballroom as though coming home from a long trip abroad. He looked as polished as his niece in his evening black.

When Anthony had facilitated the invite, his greatest concern had been their ability to acquire the right clothes for such an event. Despite his limited funds, he'd even considered offering to cover the expense of a visit to a tailor and a modiste, only to change his mind.

Such a gesture might have been viewed as charitable and would without doubt have caused Miss Quinn to turn down both him and the chance to participate this evening.

Halting in front of her and her uncle, he swept an elegant bow before straightening to his full height. "Miss Quinn. Mr. Quinn. I'm so glad you've come. And if I may, Miss Quinn, I'd like to compliment you on your appearance. You are without doubt the loveliest lady in attendance."

Her blush was immediate. "Thank you, Mr. Gibbs. It is kind of you to say so."

"I merely state the truth," he murmured, unable to take his gaze off her. For although her hair had been simply styled, the unpretentiousness of it only added to her overall charm. He loved that about her. He…did not dare finish that thought, so he cleared his throat instead and addressed her uncle. "Will you do me the honor of letting me ask your niece for a dance?"

"Certainly," Mr. Quinn said with a grin, "though whether or not she accepts shall be up to her."

"Of course. I wouldn't have it any other way." Anthony gave his attention back to Miss Quinn. "Did you pick up a dance card when you arrived?"

She nodded. "Yes, it's…um…right here, although I should warn you that I've never taken lessons. I've only ever attempted a country dance when I was little and my mama tried to show me how it was done."

"Not to worry." He took the card, considered all of the options, and jotted his name down twice before handing it back.

"A country dance *and* the waltz?" She stared at him as though he'd just told her she'd have to perform a juggling act in five minutes.

"They are the simplest ones of all, especially since you have some experience with country dances. I will help guide you, so please don't worry. And if you misstep I promise to do the same so you're not the only one drawing attention. All right?"

She bit her lip. "I'm really not sure…"

"Don't pass up the chance," Mr. Quinn told her as he leaned closer. "This is a once in a lifetime opportunity, Ada. Enjoy it."

"It will be fun," Anthony added, "I promise."

She paused just long enough to convey the extent of her doubt before expelling a deep breath. "Very well. But if anyone laughs at me I'm blaming you."

"No will dare to do so," he told her firmly. Taking quick stock of the room, he noted all the inquisitive stares directed their way. A fierce sense of protectiveness caused his hands to clench into fists. He met her gaze. "I can assure you."

Her features softened and it appeared as though she intended to say something more, but whatever it might have been was left unsaid as another young lady came to join them. Anthony immediately recognized her as Lord Rosemont's daughter, Lady Emily

"Good evening, Ada. Mr. Quinn," said Lady Emily. "I'm sorry I didn't see you arrive or I would have come over sooner."

"It's quite all right," Mr. Quinn said, "Mr... er... Westcliffe, that is, came to greet us. Are the two of you perchance acquainted?"

"A little," Lady Emily said. She smiled at Anthony while he informed her it was lovely to see her again.

"We've met at a few other social events," he said, "but we've never danced with one another. Perhaps you'd care to change that this evening, my lady? If your dance card permits?"

"Certainly, Your Grace." Lady Emily handed him her card and he wrote his name down next to two more dances. As long as he filled all the slots with other partners, he wouldn't be free for additional dances with Miss Starling.

Remembering her, he threw a glance over his shoulder and saw that his friends had positioned themselves in a manner that stopped her from chasing after him. He sent them both his silent thanks while Lady Emily mentioned her father being nearby.

"He's having a chat with some of his friends," she said. "Perhaps you'd like to join him, Mr. Quinn? I'd be happy to make the introduction."

"Thank you." Mr. Quinn clasped his hands behind his back and looked every bit the part of an upper-class gentleman. "I'd appreciate that, Lady Emily."

"In the meantime," Anthony said, conscious of the fact that Brody and Callum would not be able to keep Miss Starling at bay forever, "I'd like to invite you to take a tour of the room with me, Miss Quinn. We can have refreshments, if you like."

"Thank you, but…" She gave her full attention to her uncle. "Wouldn't you rather I join you?"

"Not at all," Mr. Quinn informed her. "I'll be fine on my own and so shall you, provided you stay in the ballroom."

"Of course, Uncle James."

Mr. Quinn smiled at her with endless amounts of fondness. "Relax, Ada. Enjoy your evening out."

Miss Quinn tracked his movements as he disappeared into the crowd with her friend, a slight crease on her brow giving evidence of her concern.

"You worry about him," Anthony remarked.

She nodded and turned her attention back to

him. "Of course I do. He's like a father to me, and while I know events such as this aren't as foreign to him as they are to me, I fear for him because of that. The confidence with which he has approached this evening could lead to terrible disappointment or worse."

"How so?" Anthony asked as he offered his arm and proceeded to steer her along the periphery of the room. Noting the frowns of displeasure that some of the people they passed wore, he sent them each an angry glare of warning.

Treat her unkindly and you shall have me to deal with.

"His decision to open a bookshop twenty years ago marked his exit from Society. Not that he or my father were ever among the upper crust, but they were accepted. Going into trade changed that for Uncle James. As far as I know, he and whatever friends he'd had before cut ties with each other. I am the only company he's kept since I came to live with him eight years ago. That sort of seclusion marks a person, Mr. Gibbs."

"So you worry he'll be out of practice and say the wrong thing?"

"Partly. I'm also afraid he'll mention the shop when someone asks about his background. He's so proud of what he's built and for good reason, but no one here will want to rub shoulders with a shop-keeper. At best, they'll make an excuse to quit his company; at worst, they'll make a veiled comment. Either way, his enthusiasm over this evening is likely to see him hurt."

Anthony considered this while keeping a careful eye trained on Miss Starling's position. She'd managed to get away from his friends but did not seem to know where he'd gone just yet. He dipped his head closer to Miss Quinn's ear and told her, "Your consideration toward your uncle is very commendable, and while I realize it might seem impossible for you to do so, I would advise you to try and ignore these concerns."

"Mr. Gibbs, I—"

"Your uncle is a grown man, not a child. I think you'll find him more able to deal with any potential unpleasantries than you give him credit for." When she merely flattened her mouth and turned her gaze toward the point in which they were headed, Anthony asked, "What of your father? Did he remain in Society until his death?"

"I suppose he might have attended some social functions if he'd been around to do so." This was said with just enough bitterness in her voice to inform Anthony that her relationship with her father had not been the best. "When Mama died, he decided it was time to live the life he'd always dreamt of. He set off for South Africa immediately after the funeral, leaving me in the care of my two older sisters. When he returned two years later, he brought some diamonds back with him – a few for each of my sisters to sell so they could improve their dowries, and the rest to finance his subsequent adventure."

"And for you?"

She took a deep breath. "I was only eleven years old at the time. He assured me he'd bring me some diamonds too when he returned from his next voyage."

"But he never did," Anthony said, getting a picture of what Miss Quinn's adolescence had been like.

"He got sick on that trip – contracted some tropical ailment from which he failed to recover. He died with less than twenty pounds in his bank account, which was barely enough to pay his solicitor what was owed."

"I'm dreadfully sorry." Her story reminded him he had to do better. His sisters depended upon it. If anything were to happen to him right now, they'd be in dire straits, with no other recourse than to marry post haste. Still, there was one uplifting piece of information to be gleaned from all of this. Miss Quinn was not a complete nobody. Even though her birthright had faded through lack of use and her uncle had chosen to work for a living, she was gentry.

He considered her elegant profile as she gave a brief nod. "I appreciate your saying so, Mr. Gibbs, and your willingness to listen to what most would deem a bit of a gloomy story."

"It might well be, but it's *your* story, Miss Quinn, and as such it matters to me a great deal."

She jerked her chin upward, allowing her gaze to catch his and letting him see the incomprehension there. Her lips parted and it appeared she was struggling to find the right words, attempting to figure out what to say.

Eventually she dropped her shoulders and told him frankly, "I'm not sure I understand you. We are from different worlds, you and I, yet you seem intent on sweeping me off my feet. Only to let it be known you're attached to Miss Starling, something I fear you might not have told me had she not made it abundantly clear when we met her in the park. And then you arrange for me to come here, for it must have been you who ensured I received an invitation. I've asked Emily and she denied any involvement."

"You're correct. I did ask Axelby to include you and your uncle on the guest list when I heard he was hosting a ball."

"Why?" She looked as baffled as a puppy who'd just been denied a treat. "I honestly fail to see the point."

They reached the refreshment table where a few older matrons were gathered. They greeted Anthony with polite smiles, but when he introduced Ada, their expressions grew visibly strained.

"Are you perchance related to Mr. Quinn, the bookshop owner?" Countess Bournerly asked, peering at Ada through her quizzing glass. She was a buxom, thin-lipped, woman with auburn hair and sharp brown eyes.

"Indeed. He's my uncle," Ada replied, her voice soft but even.

Lady Bournerly sniffed and promptly straightened her posture. Her friends, Baroness Fiddlebee and Viscountess Sillerton, raised their chins and peered down their noses at Ada.

"Well," Lady Bournerly said, "I'd not have expected to find you here."

Fury raced along Anthony's spine. He leaned toward the detestable women. "Miss Quinn is here at my personal request."

"A request Axelby would have done well to refuse," Lady Bournerly murmured while matching his glare with one of her own.

"How dare you?"

"Social rules exist for a reason, Duke. Our set should not be mingling with theirs, however much we might wish it were otherwise."

Before he could think of a fitting rebuff that didn't involve cursing the woman with every expletive known to man, she'd swept from his presence, taking her friends with her.

Anthony took a deep breath and expelled it, making a conscious effort to try and relax. He turned to Miss Quinn, whose eyes – so sparkling and bright just moments before – had dimmed.

"We shouldn't have come." She shook her head and began searching the room with her gaze, no doubt seeking her uncle. "We don't belong here."

"Nonsense." Anthony set his hand against her arm, pressing his fingers into her flesh with such urgency that she flinched. He released her in the same instance. "Forgive me."

"Of course." The words contained so much sadness they made his heart clench.

"Ignore those women, Miss Quinn. They are beneath your notice."

She gave a weary sigh. "They are members of the aristocracy."

"All the more reason for them to have better manners." Despite his lingering anger, he forced a hint of buoyancy to his voice. "Perhaps I'll send them each a copy of *The Mirror of The Graces*."

Much to his relief, her lips began to tremble until she was forced to press them together to keep from laughing. "I'm not sure they would appreciate that."

"Frankly, I find that I do not care." He gave her a warm smile. "Come, let's enjoy the rest of the evening together while avoiding those who wish to ruin our fun."

Putting the unpleasant encounter from his mind, he helped her secure a glass of punch. He took one too and drank down a mouthful before addressing their earlier discussion. "You asked me why I wanted you here this evening, and the truth is it's because you left the park before I was able to offer an explanation. While I did consider returning to the shop and forcing the subject, I decided that might have appeared too pushy. You see, as much as I wanted to tell you how things really stand between me and Miss Starling, I wanted you to have the choice of whether or not you wanted to hear me out."

"An invitation to meet you at a museum or for a walk would have had the same effect."

"Yes, but I also wanted to do something special for you. I realize it's proven a bit more uncomfortable than it should have," he added when she raised her brows. "All of that aside, I believed this was something you might not have the chance to experience otherwise. Plus, it allows us the chance to dance."

She rolled her eyes. "Please don't remind me."

He grinned and linked his arm with hers once more so they could resume their tour. "My situation pertaining to Miss Starling is not as it seems. She and I are not engaged to be married."

"But she said…" Miss Quinn gasped. "Did she lie about the contract because she thought me a threat?"

"I don't believe so, though seeing you as a threat was surely her reason for bringing it up." He drew Miss Quinn closer, allowing the length of her arm to brush his. "The fact is I went to her father, Viscount

Ebberly, a few weeks ago, when the extent of my financial troubles hit me for the first time. Miss Starling has the largest dowry of any woman currently on the marriage mart. Offering her a title in exchange for her fortune seemed like a good idea after spending a sleepless night hopelessly trying to find a path forward. So I met with her father in order to mull it over – see if he might be amenable to it."

"And I take it he was?"

"Very much so. His enthusiasm, however, had a rather rousing effect on me. I immediately regretted going to him and made it clear that I'd yet to decide if marriage would be the right answer. He agreed, but then he made me an offer I couldn't refuse, namely for Miss Starling to help my sisters with their entrance into Society in exchange for me spending time with her. He clearly imagined this leading to courtship and marriage. Especially if he's already drawn up a contract in preparation for an eventual proposal."

"Oh dear. That does sound like a bit of a bind though I do understand your reason for entering into such an agreement. Is there a chance Viscount Ebberly and Miss Starling might force your hand?" The genuine concern in her voice gave him hope.

"They could try if they were extremely determined, but I'm not sure they'll dare. Miss Starling may be intent on becoming my duchess, but she's smart enough to know that will never happen through underhanded means, like spreading gossip or placing an announcement in the papers. Although I may be struggling to fill my coffers, my position and the connections that come with it are impressive, Miss Quinn. I'll discredit her in a second if she dares to cross me like that."

"A notion you may want to keep in mind now since she seems to be heading our way."

Anthony glanced in the direction Miss Quinn was looking and muttered a curse. Well, it was time. He couldn't expect to avoid Miss Starling forever unless he fled England. Considering they'd been present in the same room for the past half hour, it was rather impressive that he'd been able to do it for as long as he had.

"Your Grace," she said, gliding into his path with the sort of syrupy smile he detested. "It's time for our dance."

Already? He glanced toward the dance floor and saw other couples take their positions for the quadrille. A brittle grimace was the best he could manage. "So it is. If you will excuse me, Miss Quinn?"

"By all means." Miss Quinn sent Miss Starling a kind smile and retreated a step so the other woman could take his arm. "Lovely to see you again. I hope you enjoy the dance."

Miss Starling blinked. Her grip on Anthony lessened ever so slightly. "I…um…thank you."

Anthony gave Miss Quinn a look he hoped would convey more than gratitude. Truth was, he was downright impressed by the level of class she'd just shown. The lack of hostility she conveyed toward a woman who wasted no time marking her territory was precisely in line with what he'd expect from his future wife.

This thought had him turning a bit too sharply and bumping into Miss Starling, who promptly gave him a haughty look of displeasure before replacing the ugly expression with something closer to adoration. Sickening, was all that came to mind in that instant. He sent Miss Quinn a sheepish look over his shoulder while moving toward the dance floor, his heart bouncing lightly when he caught her answering grin.

Once the dance was over, he'd find a way to spend more time with her, something that not only bolstered his spirits but filled him with purpose and excitement.

CHAPTER ELEVEN

Pleasure simmered within Ada's heart as she watched Mr. Gibbs walk away. Despite the blatant criticism she'd been subjected to earlier, he'd managed to cheer her. The information he'd since imparted had turned her world upside down once more. It left her feeling slightly giddy. He wasn't attached. Moreover, Miss Starling's dogged pursuit of a man with no interest in her filled Ada with sympathy as opposed to displeasure.

Honestly, she could face a dozen more Countess Bournerlys right now, and her current mood would not be dimmed.

"Did you learn something worth sharing?" Emily asked as she sidled up next to her.

Ada took a sip of punch. The drink was wonderfully refreshing. She glanced at her friend and nodded. "He's not engaged."

"That's excellent news indeed." Emily smiled. "In case you were wondering, your uncle is having a marvelous evening as well. He and Papa have become fast friends."

Despite the relief this comment evoked, Ada had to ask, "No one has questioned his presence?"

"Not at all." Emily frowned. "Why? Did someone say something to you?"

Not wanting to concern her, Ada shook her head. "Not at all. I'm glad I came."

Pleasure shone in Emily's eyes. "By the way, that gown suits you much better than it ever did me."

"Thank you once again for lending it to me. And for helping Uncle James find appropriate clothing as well. We're indebted to you."

"Nonsense," Emily said with a wave of her gloved hand. "True friendships never have debts attached. I'm merely happy to help."

"Nevertheless." Ada gave her friend a warm smile. "You truly are one in a million, Emily. Any man would be lucky to have you. Is there no one here for you to consider?"

"I'm afraid not, which is all right as far as I'm concerned. As rebellious as this may seem, I'm not really looking to marry. If it happens it happens, if not then…" She shrugged. "Point is, I absolutely refuse to settle and… Oh dear."

"Oh dear, what?" Ada followed Emily's line of vision until she spotted Mr. Gibbs's friends. They were chatting between themselves while walking in their general direction.

"I probably ought to go see how Papa is faring," Emily said, retreating a step.

"But—" The Duke of Stratton shifted his gaze and glanced toward them at that exact moment. His eyes widened and he instantly halted his progress. The Duke of Corwin turned to him with a questioning look.

"Please forgive me," Emily said in a rush. "I'll be sure to catch up with you later."

Ada blinked as Emily fled. It wasn't until she was gone that Stratton resumed his progress. By the time he reached her, the hard expression he'd worn just moments before had vanished behind a friendly demeanor.

"Miss Quinn," he said. "We're so glad you chose to join us this evening."

"It's a pleasure seeing you both again," she said, voicing the sentiment with some hesitancy while frowning in the direction Emily had vanished. Something was odd about her friend's response just now, to say nothing of Stratton's.

"Has Westcliffe mentioned the progress we've made?" Corwin asked. "We saw the two of you chatting and thought he might have told you about it."

"I don't believe he had the chance," Ada said. "We spoke of other things, but please, feel free to enlighten me."

Stratton placed his hand gently against her elbow and steered her toward the edge of the room to a spot where no one else stood. "We've almost finished the first draft."

"Truly?" When both men grinned and nodded as though they'd just conquered the highest peak, Ada nearly threw her arms around them in what would have been considered a most undignified hug. She beamed at them instead. "But that's incredible news. I can't wait to read it. Did you make things harder for the earl and his love interest? Were his sisters' reputations at stake, and if so, how did you resolve it? Oh, and—"

"We're not revealing anything." Corwin chuckled. "You'll simply have to read the book yourself in order to find out how we figured out all the puzzle pieces."

"Took some effort," Stratton said, "but I do believe you were correct, Miss Quinn. The story is stronger for it."

"And will surely be a marvelous success once published." Ada could not hide her excitement. She shared in their joy as though she herself had written the book. "Any idea when it will be finished?"

"In the coming week, I reckon." Corwin glanced toward the dance floor. "Westcliffe was right. Sharing the work enabled us to complete it much faster than we would have done otherwise."

"It helps that we had nothing better to do than

write," Stratton muttered. "I think we've put in ten hours a day each for the past two weeks. We're just struggling a bit to smooth the transitions now."

"And to make sure that it reads from beginning to end as though it was written by the same author," Stratton told her. "Fixing the inconsistencies has taken some time."

"In one spot," said Stratton, "Westcliffe had written about an upcoming ball. But when I continued writing, that ball was completely forgotten."

"So what did you do?" Ada asked. The easiest solution would have been to not mention the ball in the first place.

Stratton pushed his hands into his pockets and shrugged. "After discussing the issue at length, I decided to write two additional chapters."

"It was necessary," Corwin explained. "Without the ball, the story lacked the fairy-tale element we were trying to achieve."

"I'm thoroughly impressed," Ada told them sincerely, "and proud of you all. Writing a novel is no small feat. Many aspire to do so but it takes time and dedication to actually get it done. Especially with revisions taken into account."

"Believe me, I know," Corwin said with a twinkle in his blue eyes. "But the truth is, I've actually enjoyed the experience. I think we all have."

Stratton nodded. "Agreed. We've already discussed

writing a second book once this one's finished. The next step will likely be printing and publication."

"I recommend proof-reading first," Ada said. "A job I'll happily undertake if you like."

"We were actually hoping you would," Corwin said. "I'm sure Westcliffe will want to discuss it further. In any event he'll make sure you receive the manuscript once it's done."

"Thank you. I look forward to it."

"Meanwhile, we'll likely be biting our nails in anticipation of your verdict," Stratton told her. He jutted his chin toward the dance floor. "Looks like the quadrille is over. Here comes Westcliffe now."

"Thankfully without his most recent partner," Corwin murmured so low Ada almost missed the remark.

"I see you've been entertained during my absence," Mr. Gibbs said as he came to join them.

"Very much so," Ada said and immediately followed the comment with, "I can't believe you didn't tell me you've almost finished the novel."

"Ah…" He glanced around as if hoping to pluck an excuse out of thin air. His eyebrows snapped together. "I believe there were more pressing matters for us to discuss first."

"Possibly," she agreed. "And I'm not being critical of you. I'm just so ridiculously excited on all of your behalves."

Mr. Gibbs grinned. "Thank you, Miss Quinn. I'm pleased to hear it."

"She's offered to proofread," Stratton said.

"I would be honored to do so," Ada informed them. "And since you know where to find me, you may drop the manuscript off as soon as it's ready. I'm a quick reader too, so it shouldn't take more than a couple of days to get you my notes."

All three men's eyebrows rose. "Notes?"

"Of course. I'm sure I'll have some." When they answered with blank looks she explained, "They will include some suggestions on things to elaborate on, corrections to be made, and possible alterations to the plot."

"You cannot be serious. I thought you'd just look at spelling and grammar." Corwin glanced at his friends, his rising panic visible in his wide-eyed expression. "Please tell me she's having us on."

"I don't believe she is," Stratton said while Mr. Gibbs looked like he was ready to toss himself over the side of a cliff. "Maybe we should ask someone else to proofread. My cousin's ten-year-old son would probably do an excellent job."

Ada scowled at them. "I realize this may not be what you wish to hear, but ask yourselves this: Would you rather publish a mediocre book or an excellent one? Which do you suppose will earn you more money?"

"Your point is annoyingly good," Mr. Gibbs informed her in a dry tone.

"Thank you," Ada chirped. "I'll take that as a compliment."

He grinned. "I believe our set is about to begin. Shall we?"

"Is this the country dance or the waltz," she asked as he escorted her to the dance floor.

"The waltz." He guided her into position and turned her toward him, his left hand clasping hers while his right settled neatly against her waist. "Just follow my lead and you will be fine."

Ada took a deep breath and prayed he'd be right. The music started and off they went with him sweeping her into a gentle rhythm that forced her feet to move in time with his. He'd been right. It wasn't as hard as she'd thought, provided he led her in the correct direction and she kept her toes from stepping on his.

"Stop thinking about it," he murmured, catching her slightly off guard.

"I beg your pardon?"

He gave her a shrewd look. "I can practically hear you counting the steps and your posture's so rigid I'm struggling to turn you."

"Sorry, but in case you missed my earlier remark, I've not done this before. It's new to me and quite frankly terrifying."

"Hmm. What's your favorite flower?"

"I don't see what that's got to do with my fear of making a cake of myself."

"Humor me, will you? I sent you several bouquets but I never learned which was your favorite."

She sighed. "Peonies for their scent and anything yellow to brighten the mood."

"What about food?"

"Food?" His questions were most peculiar.

"Yes. Do you favor pork, duck, lamb, veal, or fish, for example."

"I recall having duck once when I was a child and remember it being extremely good. Besides that, I'm not really sure since we mostly eat chicken."

"And what about treats. Sweetmeats or ice?"

"I really can't say since I've never had either."

"An error I shall set about rectifying as soon as possible. It's also a wonderful reason to see you again in the near future, Miss Quinn."

She felt her cheeks warm as his hand pressed a little more firmly against her back. How could she not fall for this man when he embodied everything noble and good, his previous lapse in financial judgment aside. But everyone made mistakes in their youth, and oh, how easy it would be for her to envision a life by his side.

Stop it, you fool. He's a duke, not a butcher or even a vicar.

And yet, despite the futility of letting herself be

swept away by his charm, she found herself saying, "I'd like that, Mr. Gibbs."

He held her gaze, the intensity suggesting more than what she could ever hope for. And then to her shock and dismay he said, "It would please me if you would agree to call me Anthony."

The distraction he'd weaved with his questions vanished like morning mist and caused her to stumble. The heel of her foot came down hard on his toes, which made him stumble too, and sent them both careening sideways toward another couple.

Somehow – with what could only be referred to as immense skill – he managed to right them and circumvent the other dancers before they ended up in a sprawl. Ada coughed, choking slightly from shock and the horror of anyone having witnessed the mishap.

"I'm so sorry," she gasped.

"Don't be. It was my fault for being so forward." He eased them back into a smooth progression of the dance. "My apologies, Miss Quinn. I shouldn't have been so careless."

"It simply caught me a bit by surprise, that's all." They were moving slower than before, allowing her the time she needed to readjust her movements. "But I suppose we are friends, so if you'd rather I use your given name, then I shall respect that wish."

His hand tightened around hers, the strength of his grasp assuring her there was no risk of her stumbling again. "In that case I'll dare to be presumptuous and ask if I might call you Ada in return."

Her heart bounced about with increased vigor, leaving her far more breathless than the dance. She swallowed and did her best to ignore the immediate flush she could feel in her cheeks. "I would be honored."

The brilliant smile he gave her was proof that she'd made the right decision. She relaxed and allowed an answering grin, which bubbled over when he spun her in a wide circle.

"Would you like to take some fresh air on the terrace?" he asked once the dance was over.

She nodded. It was slightly stuffy inside and the dance had only made that more apparent. "I believe I'd like that."

"Let's go and inform your uncle then, so he won't wonder where you've gone."

His thoughtfulness and consideration left Ada slightly in awe. This wasn't the sort of man a woman need fear. He wasn't a dastardly Wickham. Nor was he the acerbic Mr. Darcy, who'd been her ideal romantic hero since reading *Pride and Prejudice* for the first time. If anything, his manner reminded her most of *Mansfield Park's* Edward, and she rather likened her relationship with him to Edward's friendship with Fanny Pryce. Even though they'd not known each other for nearly as long.

Nevertheless, she was comfortable with him and

trusted him to have her best interests at heart, to never risk putting her reputation at risk, and to offer whatever support she might need.

She believed her uncle felt the same way, which was likely why he allowed their outdoor stroll without question. It might also have had a little to do with him having a smashing good time with Emily's father, free from the censure she herself had been forced to endure.

Ada was glad to see him enjoying himself. It lifted her spirits and made her more comfortable accompanying Anthony outside. They exited through a set of French doors and strolled across the granite tile until they stood near the railing. Large torches placed at each corner bathed the terrace in an intimate glow. Additional torches strategically positioned throughout the garden offered just enough light for those who desired a more private stroll to remain within view.

A few people clustered together in various groups were silhouetted against the foliage lining the garden wall. Ada turned toward Anthony, a sudden need to know more about him prompting her to say, "I imagine a man like you, who's always known he would one day inherit a prominent title, might feel as though his life's path has been laid out for him since birth."

"I suppose that's true." He placed one hand on the railing and leaned against it, affording him with a casual look. "No one has ever asked me what I'd like to do or accomplish, and I never bothered to wonder about it. Attending Eton was expected. So was attending Cambridge since that's where Papa, Grandpapa, and all the other previous Dukes of Westcliffe went. My area of study was determined by Papa. Logic and philosophy, which I suppose is useful to some degree, though I rather imagine finance might have been better for me. Who knows?"

"Now that the choice is your own, might you decide to do something other than what was expected of you?" She hastily added, "Besides writing a book, I mean. Do you have aspirations?"

He chuckled softly while sliding his fingertips over the railing in a thoughtful sort of way. "I suppose my immediate goal is to see my sisters settled."

"Of course, but what about something that's purely for you?" Her pulse leapt slightly in response to her own forwardness. "What would you like for yourself if you could have anything in the world?"

A flicker of light caught his eyes, dancing there for the briefest second before he turned his head and it vanished. He dipped his chin and met her gaze, allowed his hand to discreetly catch hers while shielding the gesture with their bodies. His thumb stroked hers and it was as though he ignited her skin with that touch. She expelled a slow breath, unsure of what was happening right now but conscious that something was changing between them.

Time slowed. The laughter and chatter from the nearby revelers fell away until all Ada could hear was the steady beat of her heart. It was just the two of them now – a couple of friends and yet inexplicably so much more.

"You," he murmured.

CHAPTER TWELVE

Anthony worried he might have confessed too much. Judging from Ada's stricken expression, this was the last thing she thought he would say. But the magical effect of the setting, enhanced by the balmy evening air and subdued lighting, had prompted him to be honest.

It had been an impromptu confession and yet it felt utterly right. If he could have anything in the world, it truly would be her. And yet he was starting to worry she might not feel the same way. Her wide-eyed expression certainly made him doubt it. His heart gave a nervous jolt, and he realized to his dismay that his fingers were trembling.

Please say something, Ada.

"I can't imagine why," she told him, her gaze searching his as though she half expected him to retract his statement at any moment. "And no, I am not fishing for compliments, but I'm sure there must be something else you would rather choose. If you recall, it's a hypothetical question so you can pick anything you like."

"And what I would like is you," he told her, weaving their fingers together and doing his best to keep his rising panic at bay. Was there a chance he'd misjudged her? Could it be that she did not feel the same way? Had his growing attraction toward her been wholly one sided? He winced in the face of such possibility and stiffened his shoulders. "You're wonderful, Ada, in every conceivable way. The dedication and loyalty you show your uncle is admirable, your patience and kindness with me remarkable, the help you've offered me and my friends entirely selfless, and the company you've given me these past weeks has only increased my thirst for more. You are exceptional, Ada, no doubt about it. So yes, if I could have anything in the world, it would without doubt be you."

She was gawking at him as though he'd sprouted horns, which made him self-conscious in a way he'd not been since he was a boy. It was deuced uncomfortable to say the least.

And then she shook her head causing his heart to tumble, for he was now sure she would let him know that these feelings of his were misplaced.

Instead, she sniffed and gave her eyes a hasty

swipe before saying, "I would wish for the same. For you, that is. My heart is yours. It always will be."

He could scarcely believe it. The happiness flooding his veins could not be measured. It was an overwhelming maelstrom of emotion that threatened to slay him completely.

And then it hit him, with as much force as the book had hit her the day they'd first met.

He loved her. How could he not when she was the kindest, loveliest, most wonderful person he'd ever encountered?

He wanted to grab her, spin her around in his arms, and hoot with joy.

But such things weren't done. At least not without repercussion. He'd have to propose on the spot, robbing her of a say in the matter. Not an option. He had to maintain control, lest he ruin the moment by forcing her into a marriage she might not want.

He'd have to determine the right course of action. While courting her.

Yes, there was the right path for him to follow – a proper courtship culminating with an offer of marriage. Which would give him time to figure out how exactly to make this work.

With his recent success at acquiring funds, he was confident he'd find a way to finance his sisters' debuts and support a wife, provided everyone behaved economically.

There were other concerns to consider, however.

Gossip would be rife the moment Society learned that a duke meant to marry a shopkeeper's niece. Time would likely be required for Ada and her uncle to adjust. And planning would go a long way as well in preventing a scandal.

It was vital he take care – that he not rush into this like the blundering youth he'd once been. So he took a deep breath, set her hand upon his arm, and led her down toward the garden. Surely there, he'd find the sort of spot he required, a place for him to express himself without having watchful gazes assessing his every move.

"Where are we going?" she whispered when they reached a flagstone path.

"Not sure yet," he muttered. He glanced around and made a quick note of where other guests were located. Curse Axelby for planning an open garden without the proper seclusion one might find from trees and bushes.

A door beneath the terrace, all the way to the far right, caught his gaze so he headed toward it with Ada in tow. He sent a swift glance over his shoulder, then tried the handle. It was locked. Damn it.

Expelling a breath, he turned to Ada. "I'm sorry. I wanted to be alone with you for a moment without any risk of being seen, but it seems impossible."

She bit her lip and continued past the door, taking him with her until they'd turned the corner. A narrow space here offered a six-foot partition between the house and the property line and it was completely empty.

Anthony grabbed Ada's hand, moving her farther along until they blended in with the darkness. Eager to hold her, he pulled her into his arms a little more roughly than he'd intended. Her chin bumped his chest, and she gave a squeak.

"Sorry," he muttered. "I just…oh dear. Are you all right?"

She was shaking so much he feared she was crying until she produced an unladylike snort. This was instantly followed by laughter. "You seem to have a talent for giving me head injuries."

He chuckled and apologized once again while adjusting his body to hers. Having her in his arms comforted him in a way nothing else ever could. They belonged together. Nothing was as perfect as holding her close, of having her fragrance envelope his senses, of finally knowing her heart was aligned with his.

"I believe I'm starting to grasp the concept of romance," he murmured while pressing his cheek to the top of her head. "It's this. Isn't it, Ada?"

"And all the moments that brought us here combined." She sighed as she wrapped her arms around him and hugged him back without reserve.

He shifted, allowed his mouth to brush over her temple, then pressed his forehead to hers. His fingers splayed firmly across the back of her waist, holding her to him while each of his breaths washed over her skin. She shuddered slightly and arched just enough to suggest a desire for more.

Moving slowly, with every intention of letting her choose just how much she wanted to share in this moment, he grazed the bridge of her nose with his mouth, angled his head, and then paused for a second. His muscles flexed in response to the rigid restraint he willed himself to heed. She sighed, a small puff of air that caressed his lips.

"Ada?"

"Yes," she breathed.

He cradled her gently and considered the way her hands wound round his neck, how her body swayed closer, and the tell-tale tilt of her chin as she angled her face toward his. Resisting was futile. He wanted this – wanted her. Hell, wasn't this why he'd sought a private location? For this precise reason?

The distance between them vanished and he was lost – lost in the softness of her, the scent of peonies wafting around her, the feel of her body pressed against his. And the taste. He'd try to find the words to describe it later, but for now, perfection would do.

She made a deliciously throaty sound in response to his kiss, and he tightened his hold, gripping her slightly harder while moving his mouth against hers. Nibbling gently, he drew her lower lip between his own. Her gasp of surprise was all he needed to deepen the sweet caress, but the way she stiffened suggested she might not be ready for things to progress quite so quickly.

He drew back and kissed the edge of her mouth. "Forgive me. That was perhaps too bold."

"No. Well yes. I mean…you caught me by surprise, that's all."

"So you don't mind?"

She dipped her chin. "I'm sorry. I must seem terribly ignorant to you."

"Not at all." He placed his fingers beneath her chin and gave it an upward nudge. A lock of hair had come loose so he tucked it behind her ear, taking great care to keep his movements slow and gentle. "It simply means you've never been kissed before, and frankly, I love that about you. I love knowing I am the first, Ada."

"I suppose it's a good thing the same can't be said about you," she said with a nervous laugh, "or we'd never get past just pressing our mouths together."

He grinned. "It's true that I've some experience, though I dare say it's not as extensive as you might imagine. In fact, you're the first woman I've kissed in nearly a year. And while that may not seem impressive to you just yet, I hope the time will come where you will appreciate just how meaningful that is for a man my age."

She tilted her head as though studying him even though he knew the darkness prevented her from discerning his expression. "I wonder if we might try again?"

God, yes!

"I'd love to." He lowered his head. "With your permission?"

"Of course."

While he still chose to take the kiss slow, this time was different because she knew what to expect. Not only that, she proved a willingness to match his movements, permitting herself to taste him with equal fervor until they were both rendered breathless.

This time, it was he who gasped as she speared his hair with her fingers and nipped at his lips with her teeth. Good lord, the woman was a quick study, heating his blood and making him want a hell of a lot more than kissing.

He grabbed her hips and drew her flush up against him while struggling to catch his breath. "We should stop before this gets out of hand."

Before he found himself beyond the point of no return and did things he'd surely regret. It was imperative he put her first. Heaven have mercy, he'd promised her she'd be safe with him, yet here she was, about to be ravished if he weren't careful.

Lips parted, she panted slightly while staring at him. "I know you're right and yet there's the most profound urge inside me compelling me to continue. It's strange – something new I've not felt before. I'm not sure whether it's good or bad or what exactly."

"It can be both," he informed her, easing her away from his body. Her arms came loose from around his neck. She dropped them to her sides and while he mourned the loss of having her so incredibly near, he knew it was for the best. "I suppose it depends on the situation. For an unmarried couple, the feeling you just described can lead to disaster."

"Of course. I should have realized."

"No. I am the experienced one and as such I'm also the one responsible for what might happen between us if we're not careful. Make no mistake about it, Ada, I crave you with every fiber of my being and nothing would please me more than…"

Giving you pleasure.

Joining my body with yours.

Watching you come undone in my arms.

He cleared his throat and adjusted his posture, then scrubbed one hand across his jaw while trying to decide how best to proceed. Because now that he'd had a taste, there could be no going back. One way or the other, he would make her his.

"Yes?" she queried.

He took a deep breath and attempted to think of something that might cool his ardor enough for him to return indoors without making a scene. Squandering his inheritance came to mind and quickly did the trick.

"Sorry," he muttered. "I just needed a moment to gather my wits."

"Oh. I see."

Did she? Anthony seriously doubted it. He caught her hand and raised it to his lips for a swift and, in his opinion, necessary display of affection. "We ought to return to the ballroom now, but I'll call on you Ada. Tomorrow. I promise."

"I look forward to that," she said, her voice conveying a shyness her kiss had decidedly lacked.

He smiled at her fondly though it was unlikely she saw the expression. No matter, he decided, taking her by the arm and escorting her back the way they'd come. There would be plenty of time for him to show her just how much he cared in the coming days, weeks, months, and if all went as he hoped...years.

CHAPTER THIRTEEN

Nothing could ruin Anthony's excellent mood later that evening after seeing Ada and Mr. Quinn safely home. He grinned while relaxing against the squabs of his carriage and allowed himself to reflect on how well everything had turned out. He'd taken a risk in declaring himself, but the prize had been glorious.

He could scarcely wait for dawn to arrive so he could head off to the nearest hothouse. A stop at the jewelers might be in order as well, considering what he had planned.

While he couldn't afford much, he wanted the ring he gave Ada to be hers alone. Unused by anyone else. Not previously worn by one of his ancestors.

A smile teased his lips.

It was odd how easy it was to make a decision once he knew she returned his affection. How silly of him to worry what others might think of his marrying her when he was a duke who could bloody well do as he pleased. He'd show her off too, force the world to respect and welcome her as his duchess.

As for his financial woes, they would be much improved once he sold off a few more possessions. A couple of additional paintings he'd never liked and that ugly seventeenth century gilded clock that stood in the music room would serve well for starters. Hopefully, the book he'd written would grant him a steadier income once it got published.

The only minor problem might be Miss Starling. By marrying Ada, he'd surely lose her assistance with his sisters' debuts. They'd need to be sponsored by someone who'd had her own presentation at court, which he knew Ada hadn't. But maybe her friend, Lady Emily, could help.

An excellent plan.

It would work. It had to.

Because he could no longer think of a future in which Ada wasn't his wife. He needed her by his side. With her, anything was possible.

But first, a little romance. She was after all an avid reader of such books, and he was man enough to admit he quite liked such stories himself. Hell, he'd written one. Time to put some of the lessons he'd learned from Ada and her favorite book to good use.

She'd not yet tried an ice so he'd start with that.

Then a trip to the theatre perhaps, and an outing to Vauxhall might suit, with a follow-up visit to an art gallery. They could even take a boat out on the Serpentine. Oh yes, she'd love that.

He drummed his fingers against his thighs while willing the carriage to get him home faster. Perhaps he should tell his sisters. They'd be delighted to know he was planning to marry and would without doubt want to help with the wedding. Which would of course have to be small, he reflected.

Ada wouldn't mind. She'd probably prefer a more intimate affair with only the closest family and friends present. Yet another thing he loved about her.

He wondered if he'd be able to sleep tonight. Probably not with all of this energy coursing through his veins. It would be impossible for his mind to find peace since he'd so much to think of. There were an endless amount of arrangements to make in the coming weeks.

Ah, the carriage was finally pulling up in front of his home. It came to a swaying halt and one of the footmen who'd ridden outside came to open the door. He set the step down and Anthony, in his eagerness, bounded onto the metal plate.

The high-pitched moan of rusty iron snapping accompanied Anthony's fall. He pitched forward but managed to recover his balance by grabbing hold of the footman's shoulder, only to catch the edge of the pavement with the tip of his shoe. His foot slipped sideways just as the weight of his body came down on his ankle.

Pain sliced through flesh and bone while stars danced before his eyes. A strangled sound, part howl, part curse, was torn from his throat.

Hell and damnation.

"Your Grace." The footman clasped his upper arm, lending support. "I'm terribly sorry. I should have anticipated this."

"No," said the coachman, who'd leapt down from his box and dropped to a crouch so he could inspect the broken step. "This is my fault. The iron's rusted through."

"Neither of you is to blame," Anthony hissed between gritted teeth. "I was told last month that the carriage required maintenance, but I refused to listen." He'd stupidly believed it to be an unnecessary expense. All he could do right now was be thankful this happened to him and not Ada or Mr. Quinn.

"Can you walk?" the footman inquired.

Anthony tried to do so but the pain was so intense his knees nearly gave out while tears sprang to his eyes. He gasped. "It's either broken or sprained."

"In that case I'll help you inside and…oh good, Mathis is coming. He'll offer assistance."

Mathis, the butler who'd replaced his prede-cessor a few years ago, was a welcome sight indeed.

"What's happened?" he asked as soon as he reached them.

"His grace took a stumble and hurt his ankle."

Without missing a beat, Mathis wound one arm around Anthony and encouraged the footman to do the same so they could support their master's weight. Together, the three of them hobbled up the front steps and entered the townhouse.

"In there," Mathis said, setting a course for the parlor.

Much to Anthony's relief, he was quickly positioned at an angle on the sofa so his injured ankle could rest upon the seat. A cushion was placed underneath it.

"Please send for Doctor Richmond at once," Mathis instructed the footman. He waited until the footman was gone before turning to Anthony once more. "Would you care for some tea, Your Grace?"

Tea sounded lovely. "Yes please."

The butler departed with the assurance that he would return soon, allowing Anthony to sag against the sofa's backrest with a loud groan. This was not supposed to happen. He was meant to call on Ada tomorrow. He'd promised.

"Bloody nuisance."

As it stood, he only had himself to blame and with that unpleasant reminder, he flung one arm over his eyes and tried his best to ignore his discomfort.

"What's all the commotion about?" a female voice asked with a hint of playful curiosity.

Anthony raised his arm just enough to regard his youngest sister, Athena. "Why are you still awake at this hour?"

The sixteen-year-old drew closer, squinting at his leg. "Couldn't sleep. Are you injured?"

"Apparently."

She leaned forward to better study his foot. "How on earth did you manage that?"

He told her what happened, about the carriage step breaking because of neglect, and his subsequent fall.

Her eyes widened. "Why didn't you say you were struggling to make ends meet? We've so many things we might sell. My diamonds alone are worth a fortune."

"Thank you, but that is completely out of the question. They were a birthday gift from Mama and Papa." He gestured for her to sit before saying, "Don't worry. I'm already doing precisely as you suggest."

"You are?"

"You'd be surprised by how much an old painting I found in the attic was worth." He tried to reassure her with a smile. "It's not the last thing I'm selling, but it's enough to assure me that we will be fine."

Especially since he planned on reinvesting a portion of the earnings. This time he'd take better care to select the sort of companies his father had placed his faith in.

"There's also the piano," Athena suggested. "Nobody plays it."

He wondered why he'd not thought of that heavy piece of furniture himself. Its only use was gathering dust. But he supposed he'd been of the opinion that music rooms had their place in upper class homes, even if none of the family had any musical talent. It was all part of the show. His stance on that, however, was swiftly changing.

Mathis returned with tea, which was quickly poured and offered to Anthony. The sip he took was remarkably soothing. Just the thing to make a man feel like he might soon recover.

He thanked his butler, who left, and gave his attention back to his sister. "I've been contemplating my future."

Her face paled. "You're not that badly hurt, surely? I mean, you will recover from this, I assume."

Anthony grinned, despite feeling like his entire foot had been turned in the wrong direction. "One can only hope, Athena, but I would imagine so."

"Oh good." She looked visibly relieved.

Eyeing her, he drank some more tea. "I was referring to long-term plans."

"I'm not sure I follow."

He wondered how best to proceed and decided to just spit it out. "I've met a woman – the loveliest lady in all of creation. After getting to know her better, I've considered asking her to be my wife."

Athena clapped her hands and bounced in her seat. "That's wonderful news. Oh, Anthony, I can't wait to meet her. I'm sure Penny will agree."

Anthony hoped so, because Athena's sister, born ten minutes earlier than she, was known to be far more critical than her siblings.

CHAPTER FOURTEEN

Ada could not stop grinning. The memory of last night's ball and what it had led to left her with a giddy sensation. Anthony had kissed her, and what an incredible kiss it had been. She sat at her work desk with Emily's order packed and ready for delivery.

Chin propped on one hand, she stared at the wall while recalling her evening walk with Anthony. He'd been lovely – both charming and considerate. He hadn't rushed her. If anything, he'd made sure she welcomed his advances. And he'd told her he'd call on her today.

She could scarcely wait for him to do so and kept hoping she'd hear the bell ring once more. It had chimed a few times already, though not to announce Anthony's arrival. Which probably shouldn't surprise her. He would have arrived home late last night after dropping her off, so he probably wouldn't be by in the morning.

"Is Lady Emily's order ready?" Uncle James asked when he popped into the room a bit later. "If so, I thought I'd take a quick run. It will give me a chance to deposit last week's earnings with the bank."

"All right. I've got the books right here but it's quite a lot for you to carry."

"No worries. I'll have the baker's son help me. He likes earning a few extra coins."

Ada helped Uncle James bring the books to the front of the shop and waited while he inquired next door about Oliver lending a hand. When he returned with the boy, Ada saw the pair off and returned inside.

After locking the door, she placed the 'Be Back Soon' sign in the window and went to tidy the counter. Uncle James had left his ledger wide open with his spectacles on top. Various notes also lay scattered about while a stack of books still waited to be put away.

She folded his spectacles and placed them on a shelf beneath the counter, closed the ledger which she returned to its rightful spot, and gathered the notes into a neat little pile.

Once this was done, she grabbed the books and began putting them where they belonged. She was just squeezing a copy of Byron's *The Prisoner of Chillon* onto a shelf when a movement beyond the shop window caught her attention. Ada gave the book a sharp push and, satisfied it was solidly wedged between Béranger's *Chansons I* and Coleridge's *Christabel*, she approached the window and looked out at the black carriage parked in front of the shop.

Ada's heart leapt. Surely this must be Anthony.

She prepared to go and open the door, only to pause when she saw a young lady alight. Smartly attired, she stepped down onto the pavement with careful movements. It almost looked like she didn't quite trust the step to carry her weight.

An older woman followed her. The pair shared a few words with each other and started toward the shop door, only to stop and stare when they spotted the sign. Glancing about, the young lady said something more to the older woman, whom Ada believed to be a servant serving as chaperone, judging from her simpler attire.

Ada frowned. Should she go and inquire if she could help them? They might prove to be valued customers. Maybe Uncle James had managed to advertise the shop last night and these women had come to see if the shop lived up to their expectations? Oh, if only he'd not gone out.

She bit her lip. She couldn't serve them herself, but she could perhaps tell them the owner had gone out and allow them to browse the books while they waited for his return. If they questioned her presence, she could tell them she'd been cleaning while making it clear she had nothing to do with the daily business.

They were already starting back toward the carriage. If she was to act it had to be now.

She approached the door, reached for the handle, and froze when the two women suddenly turned, clearly alerted by something.

Ada shifted her gaze in the direction they looked and took a sharp breath when she spotted Miss Starling. The lady had, it appeared, just alit from her very own carriage, which was parked a bit farther along. She now hurried toward the others.

Upon reaching them, she gave her back to the shop as she spoke. It seemed like they knew each other quite well, judging from the way the young lady smiled and laughed in response to what Miss Starling said. The young lady nodded and pulled something from her reticule which she handed over to Miss Starling before returning to her carriage.

Her chaperone followed her back into the conveyance, which took off soon after, rolling along the street before disappearing from Ada's view. She pressed her lips together and chastised herself for missing her chance to invite them into the shop. But Miss Starling's arrival had put her off balance. She'd no desire to meet with her.

Yet as Miss Starling turned to glance at the shop directly, Ada realized she had no choice in the matter. Unfortunately, the lady appeared to have seen her watching, and the determination on her face now was unmistakable. She shoved whatever her friend had handed to her inside her reticule and started toward the door.

With a heavy sigh, Ada prepared herself for their inevitable encounter and went to unlock it. Intent on being polite, she forced a smile into place and tried as best as she could to ignore the discomfort she felt at having to deal with the woman alone.

Just think of Anthony. He'll likely arrive at any moment.

Or maybe Uncle James will.

No need for alarm.

Emboldened by this reminder, she turned the key, took a step back, and waited.

The door opened.

"Miss Quinn," Miss Starling exclaimed as though shocked to encounter her here, "I'm so relieved to have found you, you've no idea."

Ada clasped her hands together in front of herself. "What a pleasure it is to see you again, Miss Starling."

"Isn't it just?" Miss Starling's gaze swept the bookshop's interior. "What a delightful place this is. As an avid reader myself, I rather envy you living above a bookshop and having the latest releases available to you."

Ada frowned. "I'm not sure I understand. How do you know I live here?"

"Well, I assume you do since you cannot possibly be employed." Miss Starling tilted her head while studying Ada until she felt like squirming. "In case you're unaware, proper young ladies do not engage in this line of work. Or any work for that matter unless they're truly desperate or born into the working class. And even then, they must limit themselves to what's appropriate, like selling flowers or becoming a seamstress. Feminine things, Miss Quinn, that won't risk polluting their fragile minds."

How Ada managed to keep her mouth shut and refrain from giving Miss Starling the boot was beyond her. Nevertheless, she smiled broadly. "You're probably right. And indeed, I do live here."

"Then you've no need to live in fear of a scandal."

A scandal Ada was sure Miss Starling would happily put into motion if it served to keep Anthony from her. Clearly the woman wanted him for herself and considered Ada her rival.

Eager to send her on her way as swiftly as possible, Ada asked, "Did you wish to purchase a book? If so, you'll have to wait for my uncle, who ought to return in about half an hour."

"No, no. I didn't come here as a customer but rather as a friend."

Highly unlikely.

Ada steeled herself for whatever came next. "Really?"

"I know Westcliffe holds you in the highest regard, Miss Quinn, which is why I am hoping the two of us might get along. For his sake, that is. You see, I very much want to see him happy, and as his future wife, I'd like to make sure there's no cause for resentment between us."

"I beg your pardon?" Ada wasn't sure how she managed to get the words past the sudden dryness in her throat. She stared at Miss Starling. "You're marrying Anth...Westcliffe?"

"Of course." Miss Starling batted her eyelashes. "He and I have had a long-standing agreement. One which we cemented last week."

Ada shook her head. "I'm sorry to say this, but I fear you may have misunderstood whatever he might have told you. According to my conversation with him last night, he merely voiced the possibility with your father but has made no commitment to you."

Miss Starling chuckled. "Men will often say one thing and do the exact opposite, Miss Quinn. I'll make no pretense regarding our reason for marrying. Westcliffe needs my dowry and I want his title. It's as simple as that really. But that doesn't mean we can't have an amicable arrangement. I saw the way he looked at you last night, which is why I thought to simplify things by reaching out to you myself."

"I'm not sure I follow," Ada muttered, making a mental note to check all these facts with Anthony himself. She certainly wasn't about to trust anything this woman told her.

"This marriage of ours will be a convenience, not a love match, which has the added benefit of preventing troublesome feelings of jealousy. Indeed, I welcome your continued association with my future husband, Miss Quinn, provided you take care to be discreet."

Ada gaped at her. Surely she wasn't suggesting what Ada believed she might be. "To be clear, you've come here to…"

Lord help her, she couldn't bring herself to say it.

"Give you this." Miss Starling pulled an envelope from her reticule and handed it to Ada.

Much to Ada's shock and dismay, she almost breathed a sigh of relief when she saw that it was a wedding invitation rather than a summons to Anthony's bed. A near hysterical laughter threatened to burst past her lips as she read the flamboyant script announcing that the ceremony would take place at St. George's in less than a month.

Still, it meant nothing. It had been hand-written and might be a one-of-a-kind example. Ada would not put it past Miss Starling to resort to such trickery, which strengthened her resolve to question Anthony before letting doubt and heartache grip her.

"Thank you," she said as she slid the card back inside the envelope.

"You'll be there then?"

"I shall do my very best."

"Excellent." Miss Starling beamed at her. "So many wives make the mistake of alienating their husband's mistress. I'm rather of the opinion that one might as well be accepting. After all, there's little point in forcing a man to ignore his baser instincts or making him change his roguish ways."

Ada frowned. "I think you've severely misjudged me if you believe I would lower myself to becoming anyone's mistress. And if you think Westcliffe a rogue, you've misjudged him as well. He's anything but. Indeed, he is the best man there is – loyal, kind, protective, all of which are commendable qualities."

Miss Starling gave Ada a sympathetic smile. "Goodness, it sounds as though you're head over heels in love with him already. Which is why this arrangement will work so well. I mean, you realize you cannot marry him yourself, I hope?"

"I actually—"

"No matter." Miss Starling waved a dismissive hand through the air. "Naturally, you will be compensated handsomely for the company you provide. You'll not have to worry on that account. And since I'm sure the funds will benefit you and your uncle, I really see no issue. I mean, you have my blessing and on top of that you shan't be burdened by the daily problems so many women face the moment they say, 'I do'. Just think, Miss Quinn, you get to keep your independence, enjoy the blossoming romance you share with Westcliffe whenever the fancy strikes, and live a comfortable life. Honestly, I'm starting to envy your situation."

If Ada had been more shrewish in nature, she would have slapped Miss Starling for daring to try and turn her into a whore. As it was, her pride overruled this compulsion and gave her the strength she required to straighten her spine and raise her chin.

"I'll certainly consider everything you've just said," she told her and was grateful to hear that her voice was remarkably calm, despite the hectic beat of her heart. "Thank you so much for stopping by, Miss Starling. Should you ever wish to purchase a book, you know where to find us."

"I most certainly do," Miss Starling said with just enough of a smirk to suggest she had taken great pleasure in their conversation. "Unfortunately I must be on my way. Good day, Miss Quinn."

The horrid woman swept from the shop as though she were the queen of the land. Ada slammed the door and locked it before collapsing against it with a groan. Good grief. Miss Starling was a monster. She had to be. What she'd said could not be true, which meant she'd just delivered a long string of lies.

Ada swiped one hand across her brow and blew

out a breath. Straightening, she considered the invitation still in her hand. Her jaw tightened. It couldn't be real. Anthony wouldn't have kissed her the way he had last night if he planned to marry Miss Starling.

Of course not. To suppose such a thing was preposterous.

He'd been clear regarding his acquaintance with her. He'd explained himself in a manner that made perfect sense. So Miss Starling was obviously the villain here, which wasn't hard for Ada to believe in the slightest.

Right.

With her mind made up, she decided to wait for Anthony's arrival. When he stopped by later she'd tell him of Miss Starling's visit, and he would dismiss it as nonsense.

She paused on that thought. He had said Miss Starling would not dare cross him – that the consequence of doing so would be severe. Yet here she was, apparently willing to do whatever it took to make him hers.

Ada shook her head. An inconsequential detail. As a viscount's daughter and with her awareness of his financial problems, she probably thought herself invincible.

That had to be it. He'd been civil toward her thus far and this had made her daring.

No cause for concern.

Confident all would soon be neatly resolved, Ada went to make a fresh pot of tea. Uncle James would welcome a cup when he returned, and Anthony might like one too once he got here. She spooned some tea leaves into the teapot, poured hot water over them, and prepared to wait.

CHAPTER FIFTEEN

Propped up in bed against a pile of pillows, Anthony stared at the wall and prayed Athena would soon return with a detailed report of her excursion. Hopefully, she'd met with success and eased whatever concerns Ada might have over his not showing up as promised.

He glanced at the clock. She'd been gone two hours. Why wasn't she back yet?

Irritated by his lack of mobility and how dependent it made him on others, he considered the bell on his bedside table. What a useless tool that had proven to be since no one could hear it unless they were right outside his door.

The doctor's opinion had not improved his mood. He had advised Anthony to remain off his feet for a minimum of three days. Until the swelling went down and his ankle no longer pained him.

Well, at least it wasn't broken.

He huffed a breath and glared at the clock. Where was Athena?

And why wasn't Mathis coming to check on him? His butler knew he couldn't march across to the bell-pull if he needed something. Tea would be nice, for example. And perhaps a couple of sandwiches too. Thankfully the man had the presence of mind to send Miss Starling away when she'd stopped by a short while ago. If there was one thing his bed-ridden state was good for, it was avoiding her.

A knock at the door sounded and then Mathis entered. Finally.

He'd brought a tray with him. "Your Grace, I thought you might like a cup of hot tea and some sandwiches."

Anthony grinned. The man was a bloody oracle. "You read my mind as usual."

The hint of a smile tugged at his butler's mouth. "I do try."

He placed the tray on Anthony's lap and poured the tea before setting the pot on the nightstand. When Anthony said he needed nothing else, Mathis withdrew and left him to enjoy his refreshment. It was precisely what he needed just then, and Cook was clearly aiming to please, for she'd used his favorite sandwich filling – roast beef and tomatoes.

The meal offered a little distraction and helped fill the next ten minutes. It also made him incredibly sleepy. He yawned but forced himself to remain awake so he'd know as soon as Athena returned. A book would help.

He picked up the next Jane Austen novel he'd chosen to read. Mathis had brought it up earlier and had placed it beside him on the bed next to his lap desk, in case he felt like writing some more. Anthony glanced at the leather-bound cover. *Emma*. Not a very creative title, but then again neither was *Rob Roy*.

He opened the book and proceeded to read, immersing himself in Miss Austen's wit with an almost immediate chuckle. Emma Woodhouse promised to be a troublemaker, and he looked forward to seeing what sort of mischief she might get up to.

Sinking farther into his pillows, he read until the words started to blend together. He yawned again. Maybe he'd just close his eyes for a bit. He set the book down and allowed his eyes to slide shut. Resting for a few minutes would surely make him feel better.

A pleasant memory came to mind – of Ada serving him tea and biscuits in the cramped little room at the back of the book shop. He smiled while thinking of her and of all the wonderful possibilities meeting her last month had led to. As soon as he recovered, he'd take her for an ice at Gunther's. Yes, that was how he'd proceed. By beginning with a dessert.

He hadn't come. Ada's mind was in turmoil. He'd not even sent a note.

She gazed out her bedchamber window at the overcast sky foreshadowing rain and drummed her fingers against the sill. Something must have happened. He wouldn't just choose to ignore her like this after what they had shared. Would he?

No. She believed in him. It was imperative for her own peace of mind that she not allow Miss Starling's visit yesterday afternoon to rattle her. All would be well. He'd promised and she was confident he was a man of his word.

But why hadn't he called on her then?

Could he be ill? If that were the case he would surely have sent word so she wouldn't worry. Which she was beginning to do, of course. Perhaps he'd been hurt, but she was still positive he'd have made sure that she was informed. Unless he'd been rendered unconscious. Or worse.

She must not think like that. It would only drive her mad.

But she also wouldn't rest easy until she knew he was all right.

So she got out of bed, dressed, and prepared to go out.

"I'm going to inquire about Mr. Gibbs," she informed Uncle James when she found him at the breakfast table.

He frowned. "I'm sure he's fine, Ada. Give him a chance to stop by on his own. The last thing men want is to be harassed if they're dealing with something important. And besides, it wouldn't be appropriate, your calling on him by yourself."

"You're right, but I'm afraid I have no choice." She sat, snatched a bread roll, and proceeded to eat it without bothering to add any butter or jam. "He said he'd stop by yesterday but he didn't, which makes me very concerned."

"Does this have something to do with that woman you mentioned?"

Ada had given her uncle a brief outline of Miss Starling's visit without adding too many details, besides the fact that she believed herself to be betrothed to Anthony. Uncle James had insisted Ada speak with Anthony directly before drawing any conclusions. Which was pretty much what she herself had decided upon.

Only Anthony hadn't arrived as planned, and she was getting increasingly anxious. What she needed was answers. "I'm sure all is well, but I cannot rest easy until I know why he failed to stop by. To ease your concern regarding propriety, I'll take a few books – make it look like I'm there to deliver an order. I'll be back soon enough. I promise."

She stood, dropped a kiss on her uncle's cheek, and left after putting together a makeshift parcel.

The walk to Berkley Square took less than half an hour. She arrived at the address he'd given her when he'd ordered the Jane Austen novels, and climbed the front steps, parcel in hand. Three loud knocks summoned a smartly dressed man with a grave expression. The butler, she surmised, although he was younger than what she'd expected.

She cleared her throat. "I'd like to speak with the Duke of Westcliffe please."

"Do you have a card?" the man asked.

"Oh…um…I'm afraid not, but I'm sure he'll agree to meet with me if you tell him Miss Quinn has stopped by with his delivery."

The butler's gaze swept the length of her body before returning to her face. "The duke is not at home right now. I'm happy to accept the delivery on his behalf."

"Thank you, but I really must insist on handing it to him in person. Just to be sure he's pleased with the binding."

The butler gave her a curious look. "As I said, he's not at home. I'll be sure to let him know you called."

Ada considered the butler's words. If Anthony wasn't at home, then why had he not come to see her? An awful possibility occurred to her. "Is he in the hospital by any chance?"

"I really can't say where he is at the moment although—"

Someone descended the stairs behind the butler. Ada attempted to get a better look at who it might be – hopefully someone more willing to help.

"Is everything all right, Mathis?" The question was posed by a young woman who, Ada saw when Mathis turned just enough to glance in her direction, wore a very solemn expression.

"Yes, my lady. I was just—"

"Are you Westcliffe's sister?" Ada asked, undeterred by the scowl she received from the butler.

"I'm Lady Penelope," said the woman as she came to join the butler in the doorway. "And you are?"

"Miss Quinn. An acquaintance of your brother's. That is…my uncle owns the bookshop he frequents. He's placed several orders with us. As you can see, I've brought the latest one with me but…" Ada took a deep breath and quickly added, "He and I had an appointment yesterday but he didn't show up, so I worried something might have occurred. I just want to be sure he's all right. And to give him his order, of course."

Lady Penelope's eyebrows rose. She gave Ada the same sort of assessing look the butler had given before saying, "It's all right, Mathis. Please, Miss Quinn, step inside if you will so we may speak for a moment."

Relieved to have made some progress, Ada

crossed the threshold and the front door was promptly shut behind her.

Mathis extended his hand. "May I take your bonnet, Miss Quinn?"

"I'm afraid that won't be necessary," Lady Penelope told him. "I'm sorry, Miss Quinn but I am on my way out so this cannot take long. I merely wished to ease your concerns. My brother sprained his ankle the night before last and is mostly confined to his bed where he's presently resting."

"Oh. I'm so sorry to hear it." Ada glanced toward the stairs and wished she could climb them without any risk of the butler tackling her to the ground. Judging from the lack of recognition upon his face when she'd mentioned her name, however, she was a stranger to him and wouldn't even have been admitted had it not been for Anthony's sister.

"He has been advised to rest a few days," Lady Penelope added.

"I wonder why he didn't send word," Ada said, thinking out loud. She shook her head and tried not to feel too neglected. "No matter. I'm just glad to know he's all right."

"If you leave the order with me, I'll be sure he gets it," Lady Penelope assured her.

Ada blinked. "Oh…um…" Wary of revealing her deception, she handed over the parcel containing *Original Poems for Infant Minds by several young persons,* and wondered what Anthony might make of it.

Lady Penelope glanced at the hallway clock. "I really must be off."

"Of course. I shan't take more of your time." The front door was opened and Ada turned, prepared to depart, only to pause with a sudden need for further clarification. She turned to Lady Penelope. "I heard your brother might be planning to marry. Is that true?"

"News certainly travels fast, Miss Quinn. I didn't think he'd told anyone besides my sister." She looked a little put out, having apparently heard the news second hand. "But yes. It's true, though I do hope I can count on your discretion. From what I gather, it's all a bit hush-hush at the moment."

It felt like the ground had opened beneath Ada's feet and she was falling. She grabbed the doorjamb and held on tightly while attempting to steady herself. Her head was spinning and her stomach was now turning over. She felt distinctly unwell and feared she might be sick all over the front step if she didn't manage to pull herself together.

"Miss Quinn," said Mathis. "Are you all right?"

"Perhaps she ought to lie down for a bit in the parlor," Lady Penelope said. "You can show her out when she's feeling better."

"No," Ada shook her head and gulped down a

breath. "I'm fine. Truly. Thank you for your time, my lady. I wish you a pleasant day."

She turned and descended the front steps on wobbly legs. Miss Starling hadn't been lying. Anthony had. And Ada felt like weeping. Or possibly screaming.

How could she have been so stupid? He'd swept her off her feet with such incredible ease from the very first second they'd met. And because he'd been charming and nice, she'd fallen for him. But she ought to have known better. Men like Anthony did not court women like her. They certainly didn't marry them.

She started walking, putting one heavy foot in front of the other, willing herself to move past the sharp pang of grief she felt in the moment. By offering what had appeared to be friendship, he'd lulled her into a vulnerable state. She'd opened her heart and allowed him to kiss her, drawing her deeper into his web.

Furious with herself and with him, she wondered what might have happened if he hadn't sprained his ankle or if she hadn't learned of his plan to wed Miss Starling. In time, he might have succeeded in his attempt to seduce her while she kept telling herself they might have a future.

Well yes, they might, but it would be a destructive one, the sort Miss Starling had described as though such arrangements were normal. And perhaps they were for men like Anthony Gibbs, Duke of Westcliffe, who'd been raised to believe they could have whatever they wanted.

She clenched her teeth and stormed along the pavement, suddenly eager to get as far away from him as possible. For if today's encounter with his sister had taught her anything, it was that he was not Mr. Darcy. He was Wickham, and she'd fallen into his trap without any resistance.

CHAPTER SIXTEEN

The light was dimmer when Anthony woke from his afternoon nap. He glanced at the clock and tried to make sense of the time. It couldn't possibly be five in the afternoon, could it? Had he truly slept four hours? Inconceivable.

Apparently spraining one's ankle made one incredibly tired. He'd fallen asleep yesterday too while thinking of Ada. When he'd eventually woken, he'd learned that Athena had already gone to bed. She'd left him a note though, informing him that his message had been delivered.

He wanted to speak with her in person, however, but when he'd woken late in the morning, he'd learned that she had gone out.

He grabbed the pathetic bell he'd been given and gave it a ring. When no one answered, he shouted for someone to come and assist him at once.

The door opened and Mathis appeared with a vague look of panic about his eyes. "Yes, Your Grace?"

"Is Lady Athena home?"

"Yes."

Finally. Anthony flung the covers to one side and reached for Mathis. "Help me, will you? I need to attend to my toilette, and then I must speak with my sister."

By the time Athena arrived, Anthony had managed to wash and change his shirt. He'd also returned to his bed. He waved Athena closer and gestured toward a chair. "Did you receive a response to the letter you dropped off yesterday?"

"Not yet." She approached the chair and prepared to sit when Penelope entered without knocking.

"Forgive the intrusion," she said, "but I thought I'd join you so I don't miss out on additional news. Athena tells me you're to be married. I can't believe you told her without one word of it to me."

Anthony sighed and motioned for her to sit on the edge of his bed. "I'm sorry, Penny, but it's all a bit new, and the only reason Athena was informed was because she happened to be awake when I got home from the ball. I asked her to deliver a message to the woman I plan on marrying. She and I had agreed to meet yesterday, but I was prevented from showing up. It's strange that she hasn't responded though."

The fact that she hadn't was disappointing. Could

it be that the kiss hadn't moved her in the same way? No. He was sure it must have. So why hadn't she written to wish him well or to offer some hint of affection when he'd been injured? It didn't make sense.

He glanced at Athena. "You said you made sure the letter I wrote to Miss Quinn was delivered."

"Miss Quinn?" Penelope asked, her voice pitching a little. "Is that your intended's name?"

"Yes." Anthony frowned at his sister. "Why do you look so surprised?"

"Well, um... It might have been wise to inform Mathis so he would have known who she was when she stopped by earlier." Penelope knit her brow. "She said she was an acquaintance of yours, not your fiancée."

Anthony stared at his sister and blinked a few times. "I've not proposed to her yet but... She was here? Today?"

Penelope jutted her chin toward a side table near the door. "She brought you that."

Anthony frowned at the parcel he saw there. "What is it?"

"The book you ordered."

He hadn't ordered additional books. Curious, he asked Penelope to hand it to him, then fought to suppress a chuckle when he read the title. *Original Poems for Infant Minds by several young persons.* Ada must have used it to explain her coming here.

"What did she say?" Anthony asked his sister.

"Not much. She wanted to make sure you were all right and appeared relieved when I told her about your sprained ankle."

"But she would have known about that if she'd read the letter Athena delivered." He turned to Athena. "You handed it to Miss Quinn directly, did you not?"

A deep flush colored Athena's cheeks. She shifted while biting her lip. "The shop was closed when I arrived and then Miss Starling turned up and—"

"Miss Starling?" Anthony pushed himself into a more upright position and leaned in Athena's direction. "She was there? At the bookshop?"

Athena's nod sent a chill down his spine. "We exchanged a few words. She mentioned being acquainted with Miss Quinn and offered to deliver the letter for me when I let it slip that I was late for tea with my friend. The traffic was abysmal – very slow going on Oxford Street in particular."

"So just to be clear," Anthony said, his words measured, "you gave the letter intended for Miss Quinn to Miss Starling instead?"

"With her assurance that she would give it to Miss Quinn so I wouldn't have to wait. It was a kind offer on her part."

"No, Athena. It was not." Anthony muttered a curse beneath his breath and prayed for calm. "It's my fault. I should have told you what Miss Starling is truly like so you'd know not to trust her. Still, I cannot believe you would pass your responsibilities on to someone else. This was important. What were you thinking?"

Athena wrung her hands. Her lower lip started to tremble and then a fat tear spilled onto her cheek. "I'm sorry. I made a mistake. Miss Starling is a respectable lady. What cause did I have to doubt her word?"

"None whatsoever," Anthony admitted. He was truly starting to regret not confiding more in his sisters. If they'd only known of his problems and what they'd led to, this might not have happened. "I'll have to visit Miss Quinn myself and explain the situation in person."

"Before you do," Penny said, "there's something else you probably ought to know."

"What?" he asked with mounting dread.

Penelope's stiff expression wavered just enough to put him at risk of having an apoplectic fit. She sent her sister a hesitant glance before meeting his gaze, firming her lips, and saying, "When Miss Quinn came to call, she asked if what she'd heard was true – if you were indeed planning to marry."

"How would she…" Confused by this new development, he stared at his sister. "I've not told her of my intentions toward her yet."

"Right. I thought it odd too at the time, that she would be privy to something I'd only recently learned from Athena. But since Athena had mentioned the letter you'd asked her to give your intended and Miss Quinn appeared to be well informed, I told her she was correct."

"And?" Anthony held his breath.

Penelope tilted her head. "She didn't seem to take the news very well."

Shit.

Anthony tossed his covers aside and pointed toward the bell pull. "Ring for Mathis. I'm going out. Right now."

He clearly had a huge mess to clean up and it was past time he got started. Relying on others had just made things worse. Though that was a bit unfair since this massive misunderstanding might have been prevented if he'd not been so bloody secretive with everyone.

It was just that he'd wanted to ask for Ada's hand first. He'd wanted her to be the one person he shared his intentions with, and he'd wanted her answer before he went about telling the world. What a muck-up this was. She was probably very upset at the moment and who could blame her? If she did believe he planned to marry, it could only be because Miss Starling had put that idea in her head, which meant Ada thought she was being tossed over.

Bloody hell. He could not get to that bookshop fast enough.

"I sent a footman to purchase this for you,"

Mathis said, producing an elegant cane when Anthony mentioned his plan to leave the house. "It ought to take some of your weight off the ankle."

"Thank you." Anthony took the cane and tested it out. His ankle still ached, though not as badly as yesterday, and the cane did help. "Very thoughtful, I must say."

After seeing him down the stairs, the butler brought him his gloves and hat.

"Would you like for us to come with you?" Athena asked as she and Penelope watched him get ready to leave.

"I think it's best if I do this alone. But if Miss Starling stops by for some reason, do ask her to wait for my return." He intended to give that horrid woman a sound telling off when he saw her next. How dare she meddle in his affairs with such brazen disregard for his or Ada's feelings?

A footman escorted him to the carriage once it was brought around.

"The step has been fixed as per your request, Your Grace. It will hold your weight."

"Thank you." Anthony hoisted himself into the vehicle and knocked on the roof as soon as the door had been shut. As the horses pulled the carriage into motion, Anthony propped his sore ankle on the opposite bench and, with a groan, sank against the squabs.

Everything would be fine, he told himself, staring

out the window. The situation would soon be resolved. Ada might be upset, but she was a reasonable woman. She would at the very least hear him out. And once she did, she'd know that the only woman he'd ever consider taking to wife was her.

Perhaps he'd propose this very afternoon – forget Gunther's, Vauxhall, and boat rides in Hyde Park. They could do that later. Right now, the only thing that mattered was making sure she knew he hadn't abandoned her.

Satisfied with this rational plan, he relaxed a bit more. Athena had made an honest error in judgment, but she was only sixteen and still had a great deal to learn. From her point of view, Miss Starling was likely the essence of what a young lady should strive for. Unfortunately, Athena did not know what Miss Starling could truly be like.

Neither had he, until recently. He'd not taken her for the vindictive type until she'd made that comment about the marriage contract in the park.

He hissed in frustration and wished he'd had the sense to put her in her place sooner. But he'd been polite, had chosen to keep from causing offense. Well, lesson learned. Some people clearly deserved to be offended.

The carriage turned and arrived at the bookshop soon after. Anthony's footman helped him alight, then handed him his cane.

"Thank you."

He hobbled toward the door and pulled it open. The bell chimed, just as it had when he'd come here for the first time a few weeks ago. Spotting Mr. Quinn at the counter, he cut a path directly toward him.

The older man's eyes widened. "I didn't expect to see you again anytime soon."

Not exactly the warm greeting Anthony might have hoped for, but at least the man was speaking to him. It could have been worse after what had transpired.

"I'm sorry I didn't call on you and your niece yesterday. The carriage step broke when I got home from the Axelby ball. As a result, I sprained my ankle and have been unable to walk." He managed to reach the counter and leaned his good side against it so he could take some weight off his foot. "I did ask one of my sisters to deliver a message, but I fear it never arrived."

Mr. Quinn held Anthony's gaze for a long and strenuous moment. "Indeed it did not. My niece learned of your misfortune when she stopped by your home several hours ago."

"Yes. I'm sorry she had to find out that way." He paused, hoping Mr. Quinn would tell him he'd fetch Ada right away so they could speak with each other. When he didn't, Anthony felt compelled to say, "I also fear she may have been misinformed regarding my marital prospects. I'd very much like to discuss that with her. Do you think she's able to spare a moment in order to hear me out?"

Mr. Quinn flattened his mouth, affording the otherwise jovial man with an uncharacteristic look of displeasure. "I don't know what happened between the two of you at the ball the other evening, but I will say this – she went from being more cheerful than I've ever seen her, to looking as though she were off to the gallows. Her heart has been crushed, Your Grace."

"Which is why I must speak with her so I can make this right." He took a deep breath when Mr. Quinn merely crossed his arms and raised an eyebrow. "I love her, you see, and I want her to be my wife."

Mr. Quinn's mouth fell open. "Then why in blazes did that other woman tell Ada that *she* was to be your duchess?"

Because she's a vindictive shrew?

"I fear she's decided on something I haven't agreed to," Anthony said, as diplomatically as he possibly could.

"But when Ada went to your home, your intentions were confirmed by your sister."

"My intentions to marry *her*, not Miss Starling."

"Ah." Mr. Quinn scratched the back of his head. "I'm beginning to see the problem. This Miss Starling person should be ashamed of herself."

"Believe me, I feel the same way." Anthony gave

Mr. Quinn the most imploring look he could muster. "Given what I've just told you, will you please tell Ada I'm here to see her?"

"I'm sorry, but I'm afraid I can't do that."

"But I just told you—"

"She's left Town, Your Grace."

Anthony froze. "What?"

"She was angry and hurt by what she discovered."

"But what she discovered wasn't true."

"Perhaps not, but she doesn't know that." Mr. Quinn's shoulders drooped. "She needed to get away for a while, catch her breath and let her heart mend, without the risk of you suddenly stopping by. I'm sorry."

Not as sorry as Anthony. "Do you know where she's headed?"

"To her sister's in Hitchin."

It could have been worse, he decided. Hitchin wasn't far – just a three-hour carriage ride north. "I'll need an address."

Mr. Quinn finally smiled for the first time since Anthony's arrival. He grabbed a piece of paper and a pencil. "Will you be setting off straight away?"

"No. But soon. I've a score to settle first. Shouldn't take long though. If all goes well, I'll arrive in Hitchin before dark." He took the address Mr. Quinn gave him, pocketed it, and offered his thanks then headed back to the carriage. Before climbing in, he asked the coachman to stop by Viscount Ebberly's house on the way home.

Anthony had decided he'd start there, but when he arrived he was informed that Miss Starling had gone out – to meet him, the butler believed.

Anthony thanked the man for the information and set off for his own townhouse. For once, he hoped Miss Starling would be there so he'd not be further delayed. When he arrived. Mathis informed him that the lady was indeed waiting for him in the parlor and that Anthony's sisters had made themselves scarce.

Bracing himself, Anthony leaned on his cane as he entered the room. Miss Starling immediately leapt to her feet and rushed toward him. "Oh, you poor thing. I've been beside myself with worry after learning of your accident. Come, have a seat beside me on the sofa so I can prepare a nice cup of tea to soothe you."

"Thank you, but I think the conversation you and I are about to have calls for brandy." He swung away from her and limped to the sideboard, swatting her away when she attempted to pour the drink for him.

"Well," she said with a light chuckle, "you're certainly grumpy when you're unwell. I suppose that's a good thing for me to be aware of."

"And why is that?" Anthony asked in a steely tone. He turned to face her, solely for the purpose of glaring at her while he took the first sip of his drink.

She looked momentarily taken aback. "Why, because it's useful for a wife to know such pieces of information about her husband."

Anthony clenched his jaw and counted to three before speaking, lest he rail at her like an unhinged lunatic. A cool head was the best approach. It was vital he remember that. "I thought I made myself clear. You and I are not betrothed. More to the point, we never shall be."

"Don't be silly," Miss Starling said. "I know you need my dowry and I've always dreamed of becoming a duchess."

He could not believe her father had mentioned his financial troubles to his daughter after swearing to keep the information secret. A word with him would be in order too, apparently.

"That may well be, but it's not going to happen. And frankly, I'd rather end up in a poor house than married to you."

She gasped and her hand came to her breast, fluttering there while she stared at him in wide-eyed dismay. "You cannot possibly mean that."

"After what you've done? Most assuredly." He held her gaze while wondering how such a venomous weed had managed to thrive in London society for as long as she had. "How dare you meddle in my affairs? How dare you tell Miss Quinn you and I plan to marry? And how dare you refrain from delivering the letter I sent her?"

Miss Starling actually blinked with what seemed like confusion. "What letter?"

"Did you honestly think I wouldn't find out?" he barked, finally losing his temper. "My sister told me she met you outside the bookshop and that you offered to give the letter to Miss Quinn on her behalf. I also know that Miss Quinn did not receive it, even though you spoke with her."

"Westcliffe," Miss Starling cooed, "Please be reasonable. You know I'm only trying to protect you."

"Protect me?" Anthony sputtered, incredulous by her attempt at manipulation. Even now she refused to admit she'd done anything wrong.

"You cannot marry a woman of Miss Quinn's standing. It's impossible."

"I disagree."

"Come now." Miss Starling rolled her eyes before giving him a please-come-to-your-senses sort of look. "She lives above a bookshop for heaven's sake."

"Your point?"

"She's unworthy and will make a terrible duchess. You'll only be embarrassed by her."

Anthony took another sip of his drink before setting his glass aside and crossing his arms. He leaned against the sideboard, keeping most of his weight off his recovering ankle. "Let me be perfectly clear, Miss Starling. You and I will have nothing further to do with each other. If you see me in

214   SOPHIE BARNES

public, you'll make every effort to steer clear. Further, you will never approach Miss Quinn again. Is that understood?"

Miss Starling narrowed her gaze, her mask of pleasantness falling away to reveal her true character. "You're making a grave mistake, Westcliffe. Marry me and you can have it all – a sizeable fortune, a respectable wife, and the woman you love to warm your bed. Although I must confess, Miss Quinn did not appear taken by that idea, which makes me wonder if she really cares for you as much as you hope."

An icy chill swept the length of Anthony's spine. His heartbeats slowed as he stared at Miss Starling, praying he'd misunderstood her meaning. "You did not suggest to Miss Quinn that she become my mistress."

To even suppose a respectable lady would broach such a subject was unthinkable. Then again, the more he learned about Miss Starling, the less respectable she appeared.

"It seemed like the ideal solution to all of our problems."

Anthony glared at her. "What the hell is wrong with you?"

"I…I don't know what you mean."

He hardened his jaw, resisting the urge to cross the space between them and shake her until her teeth rattled. "You will sing Miss Quinn's praises from this day onward. In fact, you will make a conscious effort to have her welcomed into Society."

"How on earth am I to accomplish—"

"In addition, you will donate your allowance to her for the next three months."

Miss Amanda gasped. "You cannot be serious."

He narrowed his gaze on her. "You have spread lies and deceit in the most underhanded way imaginable. Be grateful that I do not demand more."

"But Westcliffe. I need those funds for outings, clothes, and other necessary purchases. With the Season still underway, it would be impossible for me to manage without."

"Punishments ought to be felt, which is why I'm choosing to make this part of yours." When she glared at him in return he said, "Should you decide to try and thwart me in this, should you attempt to hurt Miss Quinn further, or me for that matter, I will make sure every respectable door is closed to you henceforth. In fact, if even the slightest rumor containing my name or Miss Quinn's should reach my ears, I will assume it was caused by you, and in return, my retaliation will be swift and unforgiving. Do I make myself clear?"

"I don't—"

"Miss Starling," he growled, the last of his thinly held control beginning to waver. "Do. I. Make. Myself. Clear? Or will you have me drag your father into this debacle as well?"

Her eyes widened and she quickly shook her head. "That won't be necessary."

He held her gaze. "Good."

"If I may, I'd like to—"

"That will be all." He gestured to the door.

She stood, her posture lacking its usual self-assurance. "I'll bid you good day then, Your Grace."

"Good day, Miss Starling."

He waited until he heard the front door close behind her before summoning Mathis.

"Yes, Your Grace?" the butler inquired when he appeared.

"Please have an overnight bag packed for me and the carriage brought round. I'd like to leave for Hitchin within half an hour."

As soon as Mathis assured him he'd see to it straight away, Anthony made his way to his study. There he penned two quick notes addressed to Brody and Callum. His friends would need to know that he wouldn't be meeting with them this evening. They also needed to be assured that he would keep working on the book.

He'd take his lap desk with him and write while he travelled.

Somehow, he'd have to find the presence of mind to focus, despite feeling as though the world was crashing down over his head.

CHAPTER SEVENTEEN

Ada stared out of her sister's parlor window while sipping a cup of hot tea. Her mind was in turmoil and her heart in absolute tatters. She wondered how long it would take for either to be restored to normal.

"Why not come sit with me?" Bethany asked, her voice hushed on account of her baby daughter who slept in a cot near the fire. "There's plenty of mending to keep your hands busy."

"The problem is not with my hands," Ada muttered, her gaze tracking the rain as it fell against the window pane and slid down the glass in long streaks. "And sitting makes me restless. I've been doing so most of the day, first this morning, then in the carriage, and finally here after my arrival."

The only exercise she'd gotten had been the brisk walk she'd taken to Berkley Square and back.

Perhaps it was time for another, regardless of the weather. It would in all likelihood help calm her thoughts. Which fluctuated between regret, anger, and absolute misery.

"I simply meant that it ought to provide a better distraction than looking out the window."

Ada sighed. Perhaps coming here had been a mistake. She'd forgotten how domestically inclined her sister could be. In her opinion, all problems could be fixed by completing a chore. Then again, she'd fallen for a man who'd loved her in return, instead of a duke she had no hope of marrying.

"Thank you for thinking of me," Ada said, turning to face her, "but you know I'm not very good with needle or thread."

Had there been a book to bind, it would have been an entirely different matter. If only she'd thought to bring some of her tools along.

She glanced at the door. "I think I'll go out."

Bethany looked up sharply from the piece of embroidery in her lap. "In this weather? You can't possibly, Ada. Not without getting soaked through in a second."

"Perhaps not," Ada agreed, "but I think the fresh air will do me some good. I shan't be long."

"But" —Ada had already set her cup down and was crossing the floor— "you risk getting sick, which won't be good for the baby."

Ada stopped, shook her head, and expelled a deep

breath. "You're right. Forgive me. I'm not used to considering such things."

"It's all right." Bethany patted the seat beside her. "Come. There's a hem here that doesn't require great skill. Why not give it a try?"

Ada scrunched her nose but chose not to argue. Perhaps Bethany was right and focusing on some menial task would help. At least the spot by the fire was warm, she reflected, as she sank down onto the loveseat beside her sister. A petticoat was quickly placed in her lap and a threaded needle provided.

"Just stitch along the edge of that seam there," Bethany said, showing her where the previous stitching had come undone.

Ada picked up the needle and went to work, doing her best to keep the stitches short and neat, like Mama had taught her. But the monotony of the task did not keep her mind from wandering. Her thoughts repeatedly strayed to Anthony, to the conversation they'd shared at the ball, and the kiss that had followed.

Good heavens. Had that happened only the day before last?

It already felt like forever ago with everything that had transpired since.

Would he even know she'd stopped by? Would his sister have thought to mention it to him? Probably not.

Eventually, her uncle would tell him she'd gone

away for a while. In the event he stopped by the shop. Unfortunately, given how much Uncle James relied upon her, she couldn't stay gone for long. She'd have to return. Not just for Uncle James's sake, but for the sake of helping Anthony and his friends with their book.

If only she hadn't offered to help them with it. Except she had, and as such, she was now committed – honor bound – to see the task through. All she could do was hope she'd be somewhat recovered and ready to face the duke when their paths crossed next.

Right now, that seemed highly unlikely considering how much she struggled to hold herself together.

"Will you not share your reason for choosing to visit?" Bethany quietly inquired.

Ada had not mentioned Anthony. She'd merely shown up and asked if she might stay a while. "I'd rather not."

If she did, she'd probably burst into tears.

"You said Uncle James is all right – that your coming has nothing to do with him. Yes?"

"Correct."

"The two of you are getting on well enough?"

"Yes. He's a wonderful man. I've no idea what I would do without him to rely on."

Bethany placed her hand over Ada's. "Stewart and I would help you, Ada. Surely you know that."

"Thank you." Ada appreciated the gesture of kindness. For although her brother-in-law did all right for himself as a solicitor, his practice was still quite new. Making a name for himself and improving his income would take time.

"I realize Papa neglected you with regard to a dowry," Bethany added. "It wasn't fair. If I had money saved away somewhere, I'd give it to you in a heartbeat. But everything we have has been spent on this house. From what I gather, based on the letters she sends on occasion, Dorothy is no better off."

"I know," Ada murmured. "It's all right. I'm actually very content in London with Uncle James. I just needed a break for a few days. That's all."

"Are you certain there's nothing else?" Bethany asked. "When you arrived, you looked like you'd come from a funeral."

Ada pressed her lips into a tight line and forced a smile. "It's nothing. Just a bit of a misunderstanding with someone I thought was a friend."

"Ah." Bethany nodded as though that made perfect sense to her. "Well, you're welcome here. We'll make sure you forget whatever grief this person caused you in no time at all."

As much as Ada appreciated the sentiment, she doubted her sister's plan would work. Forgetting Anthony would be as impossible as forgetting her very own name. But with time, she hoped her heart would hurt a bit less when she thought about him.

What was wrong with carriages these days? Whenever Anthony used one it never seemed to move as fast as he'd like. Getting out of London had taken ages, whether because of the hour he'd chosen to set off or some other reason, he'd no idea. But at least they were finally on the North Road.

Angling himself, he peered out the window and tried to glimpse the road ahead. Ah. His was not the only carriage. There was a bloody procession of them. No wonder they were trotting rather than racing along as he'd hoped. By now, they ought to have been halfway there, but he feared they'd only travelled a third of the journey.

He gave his head a swift shake and reclined against the squabs, his sprained ankle resting comfortably on the opposite bench.

Closing his eyes briefly, he pondered the various invitations he'd received these past few weeks. There had been a couple of house parties among them, which could explain the sudden rush of carriages heading toward the Earl of Cloverfield's estate.

They'd continue past Hitchin if he were correct, so he might as well resign himself to arriving at Ada's sister's an hour later than he'd initially planned. Crossing his arms, he went back over the events of the past forty-eight hours. At this time the day before yesterday, he'd been excited about the ball, and the prospect of seeing Ada.

Now, he felt like his life was falling apart.

He gnashed his teeth and wondered if he would ever stop being angry with Miss Starling. What she'd done was utterly unforgiveable. Perhaps he ought to have punished her more. Her intention had after all been to wreck Ada's life and his for her own selfish gain.

All he could do was hope the damage she'd done wasn't permanent. Hopefully, Ada would see him when he showed up and listen to his explanation. Hopefully, she would believe what he told her for if she didn't…

Swallowing, he tried to ignore the way his gut twisted. They would find a way to get through this. He had to have faith.

The carriage trundled onward as rain started to fall – a steady pitter patter that gradually turned into a full downpour. Progress became increasingly tedious, until the horses had slowed to little more than a walk. Anthony huffed an unhappy breath.

At this rate he'd not get there until well after dark, which might make finding the house a bit more of a challenge.

Plus, arriving after five was bad enough form without also intruding on supper, which he was now sure to do unless he delayed and arrived even later. He drummed his fingers restlessly on his thigh and decided he might as well give up fretting about it since it was out of his hands.

One thing was certain – he would not wait until morning to call on Ada. He absolutely had to speak with her before he went to bed or he'd not be able to sleep. Confined to the cabin in which he travelled, he glanced at the lap desk Mathis had sent along with him. Perhaps if he wrote a little, the time would pass quicker and he would relax.

He grabbed the lap desk, opened it, and retrieved a piece of paper. Since Brody had written the last third of the novel, he was also meant to write the ending, but when Anthony had spoken to him at the ball, he'd mentioned struggling with it. So all three men had decided to give it a go. Eventually, they'd present the different versions to Ada – provided she'd be on speaking terms with him once more – and let her pick the one she thought was best.

Anthony dipped his quill in the inkwell and went to work. Now that he knew what it meant to lose one's chance at true love, he had no trouble relating to what the earl in the story was going through. He, too, was chasing after the woman he wanted and was desperate to reach her before she arrived at Gretna Green and married another. All because he'd been too afraid of what others would say if he made her his wife.

Anthony would not make the same mistake, he vowed.

To hell with public scrutiny.

All that mattered was Ada.

And it was because of how much he needed her to accept his offer of marriage that his heart gave a nervous jolt when the carriage eventually came to a halt.

They'd arrived in front of a narrow but well-kept house. Anthony gathered the papers he'd been working on and packed them away along with his quill. He grabbed his cane and waited for his footman to set down the step. The poor man, drenched from head to toe on account of the rain, completed the job without any hint of displeasure, and helped Anthony alight.

"Thank you, Travis. I'll see to it that you get a hot bath and a comfortable bed for the night."

"I'd appreciate that a great deal, Your Grace. Thank you."

Eager to get out of the horrid weather, Anthony hobbled across the pavement and started up the steps that led to Bethany Howard's front door. Once there, he gave the knocker a few solid raps.

It didn't take long for the door to open. A young man dressed in a dark brown wool jacket and matching trousers answered the call. He stared at Anthony "Yes?"

"Pardon the intrusion," Anthony said. "I'm the Duke of Westcliffe. I've come to speak with Miss Ada Quinn, if she's available."

When the other man simply gaped at him, he produced a card and handed it over, just to be sure his identity wouldn't be called into question.

"This is the Howard home, is it not?" he asked, when the silence dragged on.

"Um…yes. Of course. Forgive me. I… Do come in." The man stepped aside so Anthony could enter. "I'm Mr. Stewart Howard, Miss Quinn's brother-in-law."

"A pleasure to make your acquaintance," Anthony said.

"A shock to make yours," Mr. Howard responded. His eyes widened as though he'd not meant to say that out loud. "Forgive me but your arrival is most unexpected. It's also a pleasure to meet you, Your Grace."

"I gather Miss Quinn made no mention of me?" The disappointment Anthony felt over this could not be measured. He wasn't sure how he'd expected to be greeted, but it hadn't been like this – as though he were a stranger no one had heard of.

"She hasn't said much of anything since she got here," Mr. Howard informed him. "Refused to address whatever it was that brought her to our doorstep, except it having to do with a friend letting her down. I'm guessing that friend might be you, although I'm not sure if that means I should welcome you or chase you away."

"This is your home, Mr. Howard. If you ask me

to leave I shall do so, although I'm hoping you'll let me speak with Miss Quinn first. There's been a terrible misunderstanding, you see, and I'd very much like to straighten it out."

"I can't promise she'll see you."

"All I'm asking is for you to tell her I'm here. The rest will be up to her."

"Very well then." Mr. Howard suggested Anthony place his hat and gloves on the hallway table before inviting him to enter the parlor. "Help yourself to a drink if you like while I inform my wife and Miss Quinn of your arrival."

Anthony entered the tidy room where a fire burned with an orange glow. The space was small and the furniture of a cheaper quality than what he was used to, but it was clean and orderly. He'd even go so far as to say it was cozier than any other home he'd ever visited.

The style was simple, a little bit rougher than one might find in upper class homes, with less flamboyance about it. A heavy wool blanket draped over the side of the love-seat, a basket of knitting tucked underneath a nearby table, and a pair of spectacles seemingly forgotten on top of a book offered a glimpse of what life was like inside these walls.

Warm and comfortable in a way he'd not felt before meeting Ada.

He needed her to understand what had happened – that he'd had nothing to do with Miss Starling's lies – that he loved her, needed her, wanted her, and—

"No." He heard the hasty footsteps upon the hallway floor and caught a fleeting glimpse of someone hurrying past the partially open parlor door. "Tell him to leave. I've nothing to say to that man."

Anthony crossed the room and flung open the door just in time to spy the hem of a dove grey gown disappearing up the stairs.

"Ada!" He knew it was highly uncivilized of him to holler her given name, but he was beyond caring. "Please come and—"

An upstairs door slammed shut.

He stared at the stairs and briefly considered going in pursuit, only to change his mind. Turning to the two other people who filled the hallway, he bowed toward the woman who stood beside Mr. Howard. "Anthony Gibbs, Duke of Westcliffe."

"Bethany Howard, Ada's sister," said the woman.

Anthony nodded. "I'm sorry for the fuss I've caused. And for interrupting your meal, as I'm sure I must have done."

"It's fine. I'm just happy to make some sense of everything. Perhaps you'll shed some light on the situation since Ada has been more tightlipped than a country mouse." Mrs. Howard encouraged Anthony to return to the parlor where her husband proceeded to pour them each a glass of port.

"I fear your sister is under the impression that I plan to marry Viscount Ebberly's daughter." He sipped his drink and savored the sweet spicy flavor. "Apparently, the woman told your sister this was the case."

"I don't follow," Mrs. Howard said with a frown. "Why would Ada care whom you marry? I mean, it's not as though…wait…are you suggesting that you and she are… Heaven have mercy, have you made advances upon her?"

Mrs. Howard, who was a good head shorter than he and of a slight build, suddenly looked as though she might be ready to knock him out cold.

As much as he disapproved of lying, he refused to mention the kiss he and Ada had shared.

"No." He raised his hands in a gesture of surrender. "I've done no such thing."

"Then why are you here?" Mrs. Howard pressed,

Anthony sighed. "Because I want to make sure she knows the truth. It's imperative she understands how much she means to me and that it's impossible for me to live without her."

The Howards were both staring at him as though his head were upside down.

"What exactly are you saying?" Mr. Howard asked, alerting Anthony to the fact that he'd left the most important thing out.

"What I'm saying," Anthony told the pair firmly, "is that I want her to be my duchess."

CHAPTER EIGHTEEN

Anthony was here. Ada paced the cramped bedchamber she'd been given and tried to adjust to this fact. He'd climbed in his carriage, had come in pursuit, and was presently sitting downstairs in her sister's parlor.

She bit her lip as she strode three steps and turned. His arrival here had altered her perspective for the second time that day. She'd instinctively fled. Because—shame on him. How dare he? Who did he think he was? And so on and so forth.

But maybe she ought to have heard him out?

Maybe…

No. His sister had been clear. He was getting married. What was there for her to misunderstand? Besides their entire relationship, which had clearly been based on lies. Miss Starling would soon be the new Duchess of Westcliff, and they could live happily ever after. What did Ada care?

A great deal, apparently. She swiped an inconvenient tear from her right eye. She would not cry. Not over someone as undeserving as Anthony Gibbs. His only purpose in coming was probably linked to that blasted book he was writing. In all likelihood he wanted her help. Well, he'd have to do without it until she was good and ready. And then she'd offer it only to his friends so she'd not have to face him.

Crossing her arms, she spun toward the small window above the bed. Dukes did not chase after penniless women unless they had ulterior motives. And penniless women did not marry dukes, except in fairytales.

Good grief! Whatever had she been thinking, letting herself pine for someone like him? What on earth did she imagine would happen? Honestly, hearts ought to have keys attached so one could lock them up tight and keep unwanted people out.

The door creaked open behind her.

"Ada?" Bethany whispered.

"It was horribly rude of him to show up while we were eating," Ada muttered. She glanced at her sister. "Please accept my apologies on his behalf. One would think a duke might have better sense, but all that man seems to think of these days is himself."

Perhaps a touch unfair, but she was back to being hurt and angry and totally unforgiving.

"He already told us he was sorry for the late hour and suggested we resume eating while he waits for us in the parlor." Bethany lowered herself to the bed and smoothed out the blanket with her palm. "Didn't make much sense when we were already beginning to clear the table before he arrived."

"Yes, but he doesn't know that." Ada pointed at the door while sending a glare in that general direction for good measure.

"Dearest, there's clearly a great deal of unresolved issues between you two. Perhaps the best course of action would be for you to speak with him. It might help you feel better."

Ada shook her head. "I've no intention of ever seeing or speaking with him again."

The truth was, she was scared – terrified actually – that seeing him would weaken her resolve. If he'd come here to try and convince her to be his mistress, she feared she might be persuaded if he simply told her how much he missed her, needed her, yearned for her. And if he kissed her, she'd be lost.

It was imperative she not allow that to happen.

"He seems really nice," Bethany tried.

Ada snorted. "A wolf in sheep's clothing."

Bethany gave her a thoughtful look. "I wonder if he would look as pained as he does if that were truly the case."

"He's a master deceiver," Ada informed her. "Has been all along."

Bethany tilted her head. "You're certain of this?"

"Yes."

"Why?"

"Because he's going to marry another woman after he kissed me," Ada snapped. "What sort of decent and honorable man does that?"

"None that I can think of," Bethany murmured while frowning at the bed.

"Precisely," Ada agreed, "which is why I refuse to come downstairs until he's gone."

A second of silence passed before Bethany quietly asked, "Shall I relay that information to him?"

"Please do."

Bethany stood, gave a weary sigh, and departed, leaving Ada with a much bigger void in her heart. If she'd thought slamming the proverbial door in Anthony's face would help, she'd been sorely mistaken. She felt worse now than before. And while it was easy for her to blame the restless night that followed on the rain, nothing could be further from the truth.

It was Anthony. He'd come to see her and she'd lashed out, refusing him the chance to even explain himself. For someone who prided herself on being fair while he played the villain, she'd been extraordinarily unjust.

But it was too late for that now, wasn't it? She'd told him to leave and her sister had not returned to tell her the man insisted on staying. Which meant he was gone. Out of her life forever.

It was for the best. She ought to be glad.

Instead she felt wretched.

And since the matter had now been dealt with to some degree and she had no wish to overstay her welcome, she probably ought to return home too. Uncle James would be relieved to learn that he'd not have to manage without her for longer.

Deciding she might as well rise and see about catching the next coach to London, she got up, washed and dressed, then headed downstairs. Only Mrs. Lewis, the maid of all works, was awake and busy preparing breakfast.

"Would you like a cup of tea to start?" she inquired. When Ada said she'd love one, the woman collected a cup and filled it, then handed it to Ada. "The food will be ready shortly."

"Take your time," Ada said as she wandered back into the hallway and headed toward the parlor.

She entered the room with every intention of simply relaxing in front of the fire, only to freeze when she looked out the window. What the..? She bent forward slightly and moved a bit closer in order to get a better view of the vehicle she'd spotted. And blinked when she saw the Westcliffe crest on the side. The black carriage was parked immediately in front of the Howard front door.

Ada narrowed her gaze. This was really too much.

She set her cup down, grabbed a shawl, and exited the house. The rain had ceased, allowing splashes of sunshine to spill between clouds. After crossing the damp pavement, she knocked on the carriage door, which swung open almost at once.

"What do you think you're doing?" she demanded of Anthony, who was staring back at her with a somewhat bleary expression. His hair was a mess and there was a rough bit of stubble along his jawline that made him look all the more handsome and…

No!

She would not contemplate such things!

So she knit her brow and sent him the most scathing look she could manage.

"Waiting for you," he said while attempting to straighten his jacket and put his cravat back in order.

"I thought I expressly asked you not to."

"Possibly, but I chose to ignore you."

"What?" Did his arrogance have no bounds?

"We need to speak, Ada. Perhaps we should go for a walk?"

"No thank you." She swept her gaze along the length of his carriage. "Where's the driver?"

"I dropped him off at the inn last night together with my footman. Figured the pair deserved a decent night's rest."

She stared at him. Why did he have to seem so nice? And now he was struggling to climb from the carriage, reminding her of his sprained ankle. Pain and remorse on his behalf gripped her heart. She instantly wanted to wrap her arms around him and chase away all his troubles with soothing words of assurance. Which would not stand.

Deliberately backing up, she added distance for the sake of self-preservation. "I ought to return inside for breakfast."

"Before you go, please hear me out."

"Anthony." She clenched her jaw and squeezed her eyes shut while doing her utmost to stop the emotions she'd been experiencing for the past couple of days from unraveling. "Are you or are you not intending to marry?"

"I…" He cleared his throat. "There's much for me to explain before we get to that."

She shook her head. "Go back to London. Live the life you want and be happy. Just please, leave me alone."

Turning, she started back up the front steps and was almost at the door when he said, "Elizabeth Bennett leapt to the wrong conclusion, as well, regarding Darcy. But at least she agreed to listen to him in the end, Ada."

She halted and considered those words. Trust Anthony to use her favorite novel against her. He wasn't wrong either. Elizabeth had also had every reason to think the worst of Darcy based on the information she'd been provided. Was it possible Ada's situation might be similar?

And if there were even the slightest chance it might be, ought she not let the man she loved say his piece?

Dropping her hand, she returned to the pavement. "Very well. Let's go for a walk."

CHAPTER NINETEEN

The tension Anthony had been experiencing for the past couple of days faded. His body felt lighter, the pain in his ankle a little less pressing. He grabbed his cane, shut the carriage door, and offered Ada his arm. When she took it, joy burst through his veins as renewed hope surfaced.

All would be well. He was certain of it. Once he explained.

They started walking at a leisurely pace. The early morning light still retained a few hints of pink and purple, and while Hitchin was considered a town, it was more of a village compared with London. The air was fresher here, less bogged down by smoke and cloying fumes. He even noted that the street appeared wider and better maintained.

Up ahead, a gate served as the entrance to a small park. As they approached, Anthony saw it was only a twenty-by-twenty yard square, but it was pretty, with a fountain at the center and benches spread out along the periphery. A mixture of yellow, red, and white flowers filled the beds between the paved pathways.

"I should probably start by telling you that I am not engaged to Miss Starling." It seemed like the most important part of this whole debacle, so Anthony was eager to address this first and get it out of the way.

Instead of the happiness he'd expected from Ada, she gave him a skeptical look as he steered her into the park. "That's not what your sister told me. Are you telling me she was lying?"

"No." He knit his brow and marshaled his thoughts. It was easy to get confused with all the mistruths floating about. He had to keep the facts in order.

Ada snorted. "Well you can't both be right. You're either engaged or you're not."

"I'm not, but Penny didn't realize that, and in any case, she wasn't speaking of Miss Starling when you questioned her about my intention to marry."

"Oh." Ada tugged her arm free and turned to face him. "There's someone else then? Good lord. How many women have you been romancing?"

"There's no one else. There's just… Ada! Where are you going?"

"I think I've heard enough," she said, already walking away.

"Ada, don't…" He took a deep breath and gave up on the romantic proposal he'd had in mind. "There's only you, Ada. *You* are the woman I want to marry."

She stopped so abruptly it looked like she might pitch forward onto her face. Thankfully, she leaned back and turned. Her lips parted and there was a look of astonishment in her eyes – as though he'd just told her he lived on the moon and would like her to join him.

"But…" She shook her head as if hoping to make some sense of what he'd just said. "I saw the wedding invitation, and while I'll grant you that wasn't enough to convince me, the added weight of your sister's words did. So forgive me, but I don't understand, and I worry you might just be telling me what you believe will be to your advantage. Let's be honest with each other for a moment, shall we? Dukes don't marry penniless women without connections."

"True," he admitted, "but I plan to change that. First, however, it might be prudent of me to straighten out everything so it makes sense. Perhaps you'd like to sit?"

She glanced at one of the benches. "I think I'd rather remain in motion."

"Very well." He waited for her to start walking and fell into step beside her. "Let's begin with Miss

Starling. From what I've been able to piece together, she came to see you the day before last and arrived at your shop immediately after my sister. This, coupled with the shop being closed, was a stroke of fortune for her. It gave her the chance to prevent my sister from speaking with you directly as Miss Starling assured her she'd make sure the letter I'd written to you was delivered. My sister had no reason to doubt Miss Starling's sincerity since she only knows her to be a respectable lady of impeccable character."

"So you're saying your sister gave the letter you'd written me to Miss Starling, who then decided not to deliver it?"

"Precisely." He dropped a look in her direction and noted the way her eyes flashed with displeasure. "I wasn't aware she'd also created a fake invitation until you just mentioned it, but that's further proof of her scheming."

"She told me she only wanted your title and that I was therefore free to keep seeing you on the side. In fact, she insisted she'd welcome such an arrangement and that she believed wives ought to be more supportive of their husbands' mistresses since they can be beneficial to marriages of convenience."

Anthony's mouth had gone dry the moment she'd mentioned the awful proposal Miss Starling had made. His hands had fisted and the tension was back in his shoulders and spine. "She crossed the line by a huge margin, Ada. Please rest assured, I gave her a harsh dressing down and put her in her place. I very much doubt she'll be bothering either of us in the future."

"That is a relief." She gave him a wary glance before saying, "I don't usually like to speak ill of others, but I really don't like that woman and hope to never see her again."

"While I agree and share that same hope, it might not be so simple. After all, she is a viscount's daughter and will therefore be present at social events. Events I hope you'll attend as my duchess." He took her hand and did what he ought to have done as soon as he'd kissed her. Not caring if the dirt on the ground left a mark on his fawn-colored breeches, he dropped to one knee as best as he could with a still aching ankle, and gazed at her with all the love he felt in his heart. "Marry me, Ada. Be my wife, my life-long companion, closest confidante, and dearest friend. I love you, Ada, with all that I am. Please, say yes."

Her eyes glistened and her lips trembled. A jerky nod made his heart beat a little bit faster. Gulping and with a distinctive crack to her voice she managed to get the words out. "Yes. A thousand times yes. But—"

He was back on his feet and kissing her fiercely before she could finish her sentence. Yes. That was all he needed to hear. One little word that made all the difference. It righted his world and brightened the day.

"How will we manage?" she asked moments later. "What will people say?"

"First of all," he told her with a new sort of calm – the kind he'd not known since his father died. "I've realized something since the Axelby ball."

"And what's that?"

"I'm a duke. So to hell with what others might think. You and I will get through it."

"Your marrying down won't affect your sisters?"

"I am not marrying down," he informed her sternly while pulling her into a warm embrace. "Don't ever think that. If anything, I'm marrying up, Ada, for you are by far the best woman the world has to offer. Becoming your husband will be an honor, and I intend to make sure everyone is aware of this fact."

She grinned. "You're very charming when you're fighting for someone you care for. But I still fear your sisters might suffer."

"They will be fine. As will we. The income I've received from the sale of a few unnecessary posses-sions is more impressive than I'd have expected. My plan is to set a portion aside for daily expenses and reinvest the rest so we can start growing our wealth. I realize it's not a quick solution, but as long as we refrain from excessive spending, we ought to manage. Which was the other thing I realized." His shoulders relaxed as the weight of the worries he'd carried for so very long slipped away. "Keeping up appearances may not be as important as I used to believe."

"And once that brilliant book of yours sells, you and your friends will hopefully be rewarded with a small fortune."

"Yes, but that will likely take time – longer than I'd imagined, at any rate. Until then, I'm selling a few additional paintings. I'll also part with the pianoforte since no one ever plays it. There's a clock that—"

"I love you," Ada murmured, her smile broadening as she rose onto her tiptoes and kissed him once more.

He kissed her right back, grinning a little because of the all-encompassing joy he felt. "I love you too."

She chuckled as she withdrew and linked her arm firmly with his. "Uncle James will be thrilled."

"I hope so."

"You mustn't forget he's the reason we met. Quite a matchmaker, wouldn't you say?"

"Without a doubt," Anthony murmured, drawing her close to his side and dropping a kiss on top of her head.

Ada was in heaven. That truly was the best way to describe it. Fairytale land was another, she supposed, while snuggling up against Anthony in the carriage. The smile she'd been wearing since his proposal remained in place. Nothing in the world could make it falter.

Thank goodness she'd chosen to listen to him instead of relying solely on what she'd seen and heard. It was clear now she'd made a mistake, albeit an understandable one, but a mistake nonetheless.

"I'm sorry I thought the worst," she told him, realizing she had yet to apologize for misjudging him. "You did well to use *Pride and Prejudice* as a means to make me stop and listen to you. Clever."

"I was determined and rather desperate at that point. I'm also incredibly glad it worked or I might have been forced to hit you over the head with it." He snatched up the book he'd brought with him and waved it at her. "As I recall, books have a history of falling on you when you're meant to pay attention."

"It only happened once." She grinned, pushing into a more upright position.

"And a good thing it did or you and I might not have started talking."

True. What a terrible thing that would have been. Smiling at him, she closed the distance between them and kissed him. Her sister had been appalled when they'd said they'd be travelling together without a chaperone present. But Anthony had assured everyone he would marry Ada, so what was the harm in ignoring propriety a little?

Ada saw none. She was just glad to have smoothed things out with the man she wanted to spend the rest of her life with. His proposal, while not exactly as he had planned it, he insisted, had been perfect. She'd always look back on that moment with fondness.

Noting the lap desk he'd placed on the opposite bench, she asked, "How's the ending of your book coming along?"

"It's proven a challenge," he confessed. "I tried to write on my way to your sister's, but worrying over our relationship proved a hindrance. Now that the mess between us has been untangled and you are to be my wife, it might be easier for me to write a happy ending."

She smiled at that thought and bit her lip, her gaze still on the lap desk. If she were to lean across the distance and lift the lid, she had no doubt she'd find the latest pages tucked away inside.

Her fingers twitched with increased curiosity. "May I?"

A warm chuckle filled the air. "By all means."

Delighted to have his permission, she opened the lap desk and pulled out a thick stack of pages. This wasn't just the ending he'd most recently been working on. It was the part of the book he'd written in its entirety – the first third of the novel. And since it was to be the beginning, she decided to tuck away his attempt at the ending and start the proof-read she'd promised.

"Do you have a pencil I can use?" she asked a bit later. He handed one to her, saying nothing as she proceeded to cross out a couple of unnecessary words. She continued, jotting down the occasional comment as she read. "Miss Foley's eyes were likened to a clear summer sky a bit earlier, but they're now described as green."

"Really?" Anthony leaned closer as though to get a better look at his mistake. "Not sure how that happened. They're supposed to be blue."

She made a note of that in the margin and moved on. The carriage bumped along the dirt road, jostling her and making it difficult for her to keep her hand steady.

"Here." Anthony placed the lap desk in her lap. "A solid surface might help."

She lifted her gaze toward his and smiled in response to the thoughtful gesture. "Thank you."

He answered her with a kiss to her cheek before leaning back and letting her resume her edits. The next hour or more was passed in silence, making it easy for Ada to fully immerse herself in the story. She caught herself laughing from time to time in response to Anthony's dry wit. At other instances, the writing made her worry on the hero and heroine's behalves.

"This is excellent," she murmured when she

reached the end of chapter five and decided to take a break. "It's wonderfully engaging. So much better than your initial attempt."

His brows dipped with a hint of uncertainty. "Do you honestly think so?"

"Absolutely." She returned the manuscript to the safety of the lap desk's interior, along with the pencil, and placed it on the opposite bench. "If the rest of the book is as good as this, readers will gobble it up from start to finish."

Wonder filled his gaze. The look he gave her was so full of happiness Ada's heart leapt with infinite joy. "I for one am extremely glad we met."

"Me too," she told him, weaving her fingers together with his. She raised their joined hands and pressed a series of kisses to each of his knuckles. "You're unassuming, fair, and incredibly dashing. My own prince charming in the flesh."

"And you," he said, his voice low and intimate, "are kind, selfless, and stunning. You'll make an exemplary duchess."

"I may stumble during a curtsey."

"Thankfully, you needn't worry about that unless we're at court. It's everyone else who must curtsey to you."

"What if I trip while dancing?"

"You'll only dance with me, unless you choose otherwise, and I shall be there to catch you."

"And if I say the wrong thing or—"

"I refer you to what I said earlier. You'll be a duchess, so to hell with what others might think."

She laughed and shook her head, delighted as always by his playful humor. Leaning in, she kissed him boldly, without holding back. Her hands raked his hair and clutched at his shoulders, igniting a passion inside her that heated her blood. She gasped with the pleasure he wrought with no more than his mouth. It was inconceivable that such delight could be found in a kiss.

"What's so funny?" Anthony asked against her lips when she laughed.

She shook her head, bumping her nose against his. "Just that I never imagined Elizabeth Bennett and Darcy behaving like this once the book ended, but I suppose they must have."

He grinned. "I love that you are referring to them as though they are real people."

"Well, they do exist, even if it's only within the pages of a book."

Drawing her closer, he kissed her again with increased fervor while she did her best not to swoon. Having dreamed of a romance like this for so long, she could hardly believe one was actually coming true for her. As it turned out, happy ever afters did happen outside of novels, and she was thrilled to have found hers, in the arms of her very own duke.

CHAPTER TWENTY

It would have pleased Anthony greatly if the wedding could have taken place immediately upon their return to London. But since he believed Ada would like for her sisters to be in attendance, and since they required time to plan for being away and to travel, he accepted the eventual delay.

Athena's and Penelope's birthday, falling right at the end of the bans being cried, posed an additional hindrance.

Ada hadn't wanted to overshadow their celebration the following Saturday, so the date was finally set for the subsequent week. Five weeks after their return from Hitchin.

Instead of the fanfare generally associated with high society weddings, they had decided to limit the event to family only and host it in Anthony's garden. Athena and Penny were present of course. So was

Mr. Quinn, along with Ada's sisters and brothers-in-law.

Unfortunately, Mama was still half-way around the world somewhere and would have to find out her son had married when she returned.

Mathis and the rest of the servants lined the path the bride would travel. The vicar stood by Anthony's side, ready to proceed with the service. Anthony himself held his breath. She ought to arrive at any moment. His heart gave a solid thump.

And then there she was, dressed in cornflower blue with a crown of forget-me-nots tied in her hair. Anthony sucked in a breath and took a step forward in order to greet her. The sparkle in those deep blue eyes and the perfect curve of her kissable lips were lovely beyond compare.

"You're radiant," he murmured, a little breathless in the face of such beauty.

"Thank you, Your Grace. You're rather striking as well."

The blush in her cheeks was irresistible. Leaning in, he kissed her cheek then offered his arm and led her the last few steps to where the vicar stood waiting.

Taking turns, they made their vows. Despite a couple of hymns and the scripture the vicar elected to read, the service did not last as long as Anthony feared it might. He turned to Ada – his wife and duchess – a little dismayed by the sting in his eyes.

She beamed at him and he saw that she too was overcome by emotion. The tears gathering near her lashes spilled over at the exact same time as his.

Grinning, he pulled her into his arms and kissed her, long and deep and with the unspoken promise that he'd make her just as happy as she was right now for the rest of her life.

Since Ada's family had been invited to stay at Westcliffe house during their visit to London and Anthony's sisters also lived there, Ada and Anthony had agreed to spend their wedding night at Mivart's. The hotel, which had been established in 1812 and located at the corner of Brook and Davies streets, was known for its top-notch cuisine and exclusive clientele.

Despite Ada saying that they could forego the expense, Anthony had insisted, and she'd not been able to talk him out of it. For which she was rather glad, she decided, while lounging on the velvet sofa that stood in their suite of rooms.

The half-empty bottle of champagne they'd shared still sat in its silver ice bucket while the trays they'd picnicked from on the floor had been placed on top of the dresser. Ada's silk slippers lay near a chair where she'd toed them off the moment she and Anthony were alone. His shoes had been kicked to one side, his discarded jacket flung over the back of a chair.

She tracked his movements as he grabbed the champagne and refilled her glass. "Did you and your friends agree on the ending you'd like to use for your novel?"

"Yes," he said as he gave her the glass. "You didn't make it easy for us, but I rather like the way it turned out."

Moving her legs to make space beside her, she sipped the bubbly drink and nodded. He wasn't wrong. After reading all three endings, it had been impossible for her to choose. Each one was perfect in its own way, but upon closer reflection, she'd realized there was a reason for this. Each had a magical touch, so her suggestion had been to combine them.

"Does that mean it's finished?" she asked, meeting his gaze with a hopeful smile.

"It does." Instead of sitting, he retrieved a dark blue silk box tied with a cream-colored bow and placed it on a nearby table. "This is for you – the final edition."

Ada's heart leapt. "Anthony…"

"I encourage you to read it," he told her. "And to let me know what you think. Tomorrow."

"Tomorrow?"

"Precisely." He closed his hand around hers, pulled her to her feet, and took the glass she'd been holding, which he placed beside the box. "There are more pressing matters for us to attend to right now."

"What could possibly be more pressing tha—" Her eyes widened as he drew her flush up against him. "Oh!"

A wolfish smile told her she might as well put off all plans to read for the moment. Her husband was right. There were indeed more pressing matters, like all the tiny ridiculous buttons holding her gown in place, and the intricate knot some evil creature had made of Anthony's cravat.

"Mind if I ruin this gown?" he asked while kissing his way down her neck.

"Only if you've no intention of seeing me in it again," she sighed. "I'm abysmal with a needle and thread. Just ask my sister. She had a—"

A ripping sound accompanied the ping of a hundred small buttons dancing all over the room. Cool air caressed her skin as Anthony pushed the cap sleeves aside, sending swaths of lace-covered silk to the floor.

Ada gulped. She only wore her chemise, stays, and stockings now. But judging from the gleam in Anthony's eyes, that wasn't a bad thing. Her pulse quickened. Perhaps she ought to reciprocate?

Her gaze slid sideways, searching for something until…

She moved to the desk along one wall and snatched up a letter opener. Anthony's eyes widened.

He held up his hands and took a step back. "What's your plan, Ada?"

"To get you out of those clothes."

His horrified expression from seconds ago transformed with a laugh. "Very well, though I'm not sure what you hope to accomplish with a letter opener. They're not that sharp."

"It's not the sharpness I require." She moved toward him, raised her hand, and instantly saw apprehension return to his face even though he made an effort to hide it. "I promise not to hurt you, my love. Please trust me."

"I do," he said, and her heart melted all the more because he agreed to do so despite his concerns.

"All I want is to nudge this knot open. After that, I'll use my fingers." She pried the tip of the letter opener into a teensy tiny gap in the linen. "One would think this was tied by someone who did not want you to take it off. Is your valet really that diabolical?"

"I don't have a valet." He cleared his throat and spoke while she worked. "I've been dressing myself for years, Ada. So I tied this one just as I've tied a thousand others. But I was nervous today and may have used added strength to make certain it wouldn't unravel."

She pressed her lips together and willed herself not to laugh. He was simply too adorable for words. So she kept her gaze on his neck and told him honestly, "I was nervous too. More than I've been before in my life. It's a relief to know I wasn't alone."

"How about now?" he asked when she finally managed to pull one edge of his cravat loose. "Are you still nervous?"

"A little," she whispered, then amended that statement by admitting, "quite a bit, if I'm being perfectly honest."

His fingertips found the curve of her neck and trailed over her shoulder. "Don't be."

She shivered in response to his touch and the sizzling effect it had on her nerves. Her stomach tightened even as she managed to undo the rest of the knot at his throat. "That's easy for you to say. You've done this before, have you not?"

"If you are referring to getting naked and tupping a woman, then yes, I have. But I've never considered what she might think of my physical appearance or worried whether or not her experience would be a memorable one. It was just a need that had to be sated. But with you it's entirely different. With you my heart is racing a million miles per second and I constantly feel like I'm breaking out in a sweat. I worry I'll disappoint you, which is something I've never considered with any previous partner."

His honesty was humbling and put her more at ease. It helped knowing she wasn't the only one who felt like a novice, even if he did have the experience she lacked. "If the kisses we've shared are any indication, I'm sure I'll be more than pleased by your efforts."

She pulled the length of white linen from around his neck and barely managed to toss it aside before he kissed her with wild abandon, wrapping her tightly in his arms and pulling her close. His palms flattened over her spine, pushing heat under her skin and increasing her need for something more.

Getting him out of his waistcoat and shirt would be an excellent start, she decided when he went to work on her stays. So she broke their kiss and leaned back, catching his smoldering gaze as she started undoing his waistcoat buttons. Her stays fell forward and she pulled her arms free so the garment could be tossed aside. His waistcoat followed and then she was tugging his shirt loose from his trousers while he began to bunch her chemise.

His nails scraped her thighs, sending a series of sizzling sparks over her flesh. She gasped and he chuckled while bending to press scorching kisses against the curve of her neck. The thin lawn fabric of her chemise fluttered against her stomach as it was hitched higher.

Eager to see what her husband looked like in a state of undress, she pushed him back slightly so she could wrestle his shirt over his head. Laughing, he helped her free his arms and even managed to send her chemise flying in the process.

His eyes widened while Ada took a sharp breath,

her fingers tentatively reaching and trailing over the firm chest before her. He shivered slightly beneath her touch. She felt his heart leap as she pressed her palm to it, and when she traced the hard bands of muscle comprising his stomach, they flexed in response.

"You're stunning," she whispered while letting her gaze roam over his powerful arms before dipping back down to his narrow waist. "I never imagined…"

"Neither did I." His voice mirrored her awe and her gaze snapped to his. She'd been so distracted by his perfection she'd completely forgotten that she stood before him, completely naked, except for her stockings.

Self-awareness rushed through her and she instinctively raised her arms.

"No," he murmured, catching her wrists before she could shield herself from his view. "There will be none of that, Ada."

"But—"

"You're everything I desire and so much more. Don't hide that from me, my love. Revel in it." As if to lend encouragement, he undid his placket and took off his trousers and smalls. A roguish grin tugged at his lips. "See?"

She sucked in a breath. "Oh my."

"Precisely the sort of response I hoped to receive," he teased as he swept her into his arms. He strode to the adjoining room where a lovely canopy bed dressed in white linen waited.

A deep kiss followed as he lowered her onto the bed. He settled himself beside her, his fingers gently exploring her while his mouth coaxed her into a restless state of inexplicable need. She sighed, a little embarrassed by what she suddenly wanted – his hands, everywhere.

Shifting, she tried to adjust her position so he'd be encouraged to touch her in the right places. Instead, the wicked man merely chuckled against her shoulder and playfully nipped her with his teeth.

He added a soothing kiss. "I wonder what you desire."

The urge to smack him was equal to her wish for him to continue with his seduction. For that was surely what the annoying man was about. Either that, or he meant to drive her mad.

"Anthony," she implored. Abandoning all her scruples, she allowed her legs to fall open.

"Yes, my love?" His hand found her ankle and began sliding upward. "Is this what you're after?"

"Not quite."

"How about this?" he asked while stroking her knee.

"No." Frustrated, she curled her hand behind his head and drew him in for a deep and unyielding kiss before desperately whispering against his lips, "Please put me out of my misery."

Holding her gaze, he granted her wish, sweeping her into a maelstrom of new and powerful sensations. She moaned in response to the exquisite pleasure and clutched at his shoulders with increased force as the fire he'd stoked became an inferno.

A gasp was her first response. But as wave after wave of bliss swept through her, she cried out his name and gripped him harder. His mouth found hers once more and he kissed her deeply while settling his body between her thighs.

Then, distracting her with additional pleasure, he joined his body with hers.

What followed was without doubt the most glorious experience of Ada's life. If she'd thought the ecstasy Anthony had bestowed a few seconds before was incredible, it was nothing compared to the feeling of being one with the man she loved.

Each move they made told a story of unity, friendship, love, and devotion. It was so achingly beautiful – intimate in a way nothing else could be – and made her feel closer to him than she'd ever felt to anyone else in her life. It cut down the last remaining barriers between them and bound them together so tightly she felt their souls meld.

"Promise we'll do this as often as possible," she said a while later while snuggling against his side. Heavens, she'd never felt so languid before.

"Nothing would please me more," he told her, the

arm he'd wound around her tightening slightly. "If you like, we can continue right now."

"It's not too soon?"

"Only if you're sore."

She considered that for a second. "I think I'm all right."

"In that case..." Before she could blink, he'd rolled her onto his outstretched body. "I'm more than happy to further your education, Your Grace."

He waggled his eyebrows and Ada grinned. "Really?"

"Allow me to demonstrate," he told her in a seductive tone.

And so he did, until she was breathless once more.

CHAPTER TWENTY-ONE

A s had become the norm, Harriet Michaels got
up at three. With work commencing at four,
she'd barely managed to squeeze in her usual five
hours of sleep before the knocker-upper tapped his
rod against her window. She scrambled from the
bed, sent him a quick wave of thanks, and went to
heat a pot of water on the small range that stood in
the corner of the room.

Her younger sister, Lucy, who was twelve years
of age, wouldn't be up for a while yet. But when she
woke, Harriet wanted her to find a pot of tea waiting
along with a bread roll, even if neither would be very
fresh by that time.

Returning to her own side of the small, one-
room accommodation she'd managed to acquire,
Harriet collected the clothes she'd left on a nearby
chair last night and began putting them on. She had

only a few sets to choose between, and laundry was something she couldn't afford too often. So she did her best to keep her attire in decent order, even though it was often a challenge to keep ink stains off.

Having finished with her bindings, she put on her shirt and trousers, then tied her cravat. Next, she slipped on her waistcoat, which she quickly buttoned before pushing her arms through the sleeves of her brown tweed jacket. Hose and shoes followed.

To finish off the ensemble, she pressed a cap onto her head.

Turning toward the small tarnished mirror that hung on the wall, she took a moment to study her appearance – to make sure she looked the part she'd decided to play.

A scrawny boy stared back, offering no hint of feminine features or curves whatsoever.

Perfect.

Satisfied she would avoid detection once more, Harriet went to prepare the tea. She made a cup for herself first, then let it cool for the five minutes it took her to run downstairs and purchase a couple of bread rolls from the baker up the street.

She ate half of hers on the way back to her lodgings and left the other on a plate for Lucy to find later. The tea was a bit thin as usual, but it was hot and hit the spot nicely, washing down her simple breakfast. Ready to leave, Harriet crossed to her sister's bed, knelt down, and pressed a tender kiss to her brow.

"I'll see you later, dearest," she whispered.

Her sister, a deep sleeper since birth, didn't budge.

Harriet straightened, blew her a kiss, and left the room, locking the door behind her. After exiting the building, she turned left and headed toward Holborn. From there it was a three mile walk to Hudson & Co and the printing press where she'd spend the next fourteen hours filling composing sticks with sorts.

Moving briskly with the soles of her shoes slapping the pavement, she passed a newspaper boy and smiled when she spotted the headline on one of the papers he carried. 'The Duke of Westcliffe Marries For Love' it read.

Although she'd not managed to speak with Ada after her wedding, she had sent a card congratulating her on her nuptials. Harriet was happy on her friend's behalf and looked forward to telling her so in person during their next book club meeting.

It pleased her to know that happily ever afters were possible even when they seemed unlikely. She herself had lost all hope of marrying for any reason, never mind love, a long time ago. But if she applied herself properly, there might be a chance for Lucy.

With this in mind, she rounded the street

corner with increased speed, only to have her shoulder knocked back as it bumped into something solid that came from the opposite direction. She grunted in response to the impact and opened her mouth with every intention of voicing an apology to the man she'd walked into. But when she raised her gaze and was met by a pair of ocean blue eyes, the words she'd intended to speak caught in her throat.

The gentleman, impeccably dressed in a perfectly tailored outfit consisting of black tailcoat, ivory waistcoat, and fawn-colored trousers, was also incredibly handsome. And tall. She had to crane her neck to see his dark blonde locks peeking out from beneath the brim of his elegant hat. A square jaw served to highlight his masculine looks, which were perfectly offset by a full-bodied mouth and a slender nose.

Surprise made her blink. What on earth was such a fine gentleman doing out and about at this early hour?

He jerked his chin and touched the brim of his hat. "Excuse me."

That was all he said before he stepped past her, continuing onward while Harriet simply stood there, staring at his retreating back until some other passerby happened to jostle her.

"Get out of the way, lad," said a stocky man with a crate perched on his shoulder.

Harriet leapt to one side, gave her head a quick shake, and resumed walking.

Ninny.

Her silly heart fluttered and her body felt lighter. All because of a stranger. A very attractive one to be sure, but one she'd never cross paths with again. And even if she did, he'd remain unattainable.

They were from two different worlds. Their lives would never align.

Ready for the sequel? *A Duke's Introduction to Courtship* is a secret identities workplace romance that I'm sure you'll love!

Order your copy today, and sign up for my newsletter at www.sophiebarnes.com so you don't miss out on my freebies, special deals, and giveaways. You'll receive a complimentary copy of *No Ordinary Duke* with your subscription!

Did you enjoy *A Duke's Guide to Romance*? If so, please take a moment to leave a review since this can help other readers discover books they'll love.

Keep turning for my author's note and additional information on A Duke's Introduction to Courtship.

Read the next book in the series!

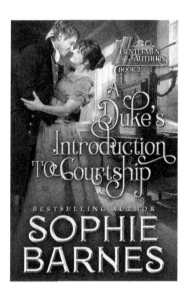

Love caught him completely off guard and forced him to question everything...

When Brody Evans, Duke of Corwin, goes incognito at a printing press, he doesn't anticipate meeting Mr. Michaels, a charming young man with whom he shares an instant connection. Soon he's questioning everything he believed to be true of himself, while losing his heart in the process. Accepting the way he feels is not only hard, it's also illegal and downright dangerous. Until he learns the truth and is forced to wonder whether or not the person he fell for is real, or just an illusion.

Dressed as a boy, Harriet Michaels acquires a job at a printing press so she can support herself and her younger sister. It seems like a good idea until she meets Mr. Evans, the new assistant editor. Her attraction toward him cannot be denied, but it must be concealed if she's to avoid detection and the risk of losing her job. The more time she spends with him, however, the closer she comes to heartache and ruin. For as it turns out, Mr. Evans is not who he claims to be either.

Order your copy today!

AUTHOR'S NOTE

Dear Reader,

I hope you've enjoyed the first installment of my Gentlemen Authors series. Contrary to what this book may suggest, writing did not provide Jane Austen with much of a fortune. She received only £684 from the four books she published during her lifetime, an amount that is roughly equivalent to £74,968 today. The rights to *Pride and Prejudice* were sold to Egerton for a mere £110, a deal that appears to have been far more beneficial to the publisher than it was to Jane Austen.

However, given the great success of Jane Austen's books in the early part of the 1800s and onward, one would suppose that Ada Quinn might imagine them earning the author a larger income. Especially since other authors contemporary of Austen did make a good living with their writing.

Maria Edgeworth, for example, received £2100 for her novel, *Patronage*, while Sir Walter Scott reputedly earned an astounding income of £17,910 in 1823 alone. It's noted that he was able to amass a fortune of roughly £50,000 with which to pay off his creditors, within the span of six years.

This is of course the kind of success Anthony and his friends hope to acquire. Whether or not they'll manage remains to be seen.

Sophie
xoxo

ACKNOWLEDGMENTS

I would like to thank the Killion Group for their incredible help with the editing and cover design for this book.

And to my friends and family, thank you for your constant support and for believing in me. I would be lost without you!

ABOUT THE AUTHOR

USA TODAY bestselling author Sophie Barnes is best known for her historical romance novels in which the characters break away from social expectations in their quest for happiness and love. Having written for Avon, an imprint of Harper Collins, her books have been published internationally in eight languages.

With a fondness for travel, Sophie has lived in six countries, on three continents, and speaks English, Danish, French, Spanish, and Romanian with varying degrees of fluency. Ever the romantic, she married the same man three times—in three different countries and in three different dresses.

When she's not busy dreaming up her next swoon worthy romance novel, Sophie enjoys spending time with her family, practicing yoga, baking, gardening, watching romantic comedies and, of course, reading.

You can contact her through her website at www. sophiebarnes.com

For all the latest releases, promotions, and exclu-

sive story updates, subscribe to Sophie Barnes'
newsletter today!

And please consider leaving a review for this
book.

Every review is greatly appreciated!